THE UNWORTHY WIFE

BONZAI
MOON

BonzaiMoon Books LLC
Houston, Texas
www.bonzaimoonbooks.com

ISBN 978-1-943685-12-7 (Print)

ISBN 978-1-943685-15-8 (Large Print)

Thank you God for creative ideas! Thanks Angel Vane for being a great friend and co-writing partner! This book is dedicated to all the wonderful people I've met throughout my travels in the Caribbean!
-Rachel Woods

Thanks to Rachel for being the best co-author ever.
-Angel Vane

Rachel Woods has been entertaining readers with her brand of romantic mystery suspense -- sexy dangerous fiction. Now you can get one of her short stories for FREE, when you sign up to join her newsletter:

GET MY FREE SHORT STORY NOW

https://BookHip.com/HAGPDF

Prologue

The first time I hit him in the head with a shovel, he was surprised, shocked, stunned.

As he turned toward me, his eyes were wide and confused. I almost felt sorry for him. But not quite. Not so sorry that I wouldn't kill him. Because I had to. He had to die. And he knew why. He knew exactly what he'd done.

I swung the shovel again, connecting with the side of his head.

Crying out in shock and pain, he stumbled to one knee.

"I can't let you live," I told him. "Not after what you did ..."

I whacked him again, a resounding *thwack* that put him face down on the floor and shut him up. Sprawled on the carpet, he didn't move. Was he dead? Or, just unconscious? Maybe he was just pretending to be dead?

Just in case, I decided to hit him again. The crunch of bone and the spray of blood and brain matter comforted me.

I was convinced that he wouldn't get up because I knew he couldn't.

The son of a bitch was dead.

Chapter One

What the hell was that bitch doing here?

Noelle Bean lost her train of thought as she stared at Helen Farber. Moments ago, glancing from left to right, she'd been trying to gauge the interest of her audience when she'd seen the bitchy, bitter old hag. Her sour face twisted in a smug scowl, Helen sat in the center of the two hundred students crowded into the tiered seating of the small lecture hall.

Clearing her throat, Noelle glanced down at her notes to regain her focus. She had to finish the lecture. As an adjunct professor at the University of St. Killian's School of Pharmacy, she wasn't supposed to trail off mid-sentence and spaz out. She wasn't known for going off on tangents like most of the stodgy, musty old professors who populated the classrooms and lecture halls throughout the Colonial buildings sprawled across the five-acre campus.

Many students looked to Noelle as a mentor, even though at thirty years old she was more like a dorm R.A., and a few had told her she was an inspiration. She was a dedicated, accomplished pharmacist at Palmchat Pharmacy, the premier pharmacy chain of the Palmchat Islands, bringing dedication, knowledge, and practical skills to the classroom.

What would her students think if she fell apart because of that crazy bitch Helen Farber?

Noelle raised her gaze to the students eager for her to continue. Quickly, she scanned the sea of faces staring down at her in rapt attention, fingers poised over smart tablets and laptops as they continued to wait.

Taking a small breath, Noelle spotted six or seven students clustered in three rows on the right side of the hall. Thankful for familiar faces, she focused on the doctoral students, each in their final year of the pharmacy college—Tina Chen-Soo, Sarah Linde, Matt Delany, Kevin Cook, Jimmy Quible and Eamon Taylor. The six had recently completed the Palmchat Pharmacy Company's Internship Program. Highly prestigious and extremely competitive, the program was designed to give fourth-year doctoral students an on-the-job retail pharmacy experience.

Noelle had been chosen as the Intern Mentor of the current cohort, a coveted position within the company. Not only was she tasked with supervision and guidance, but at the end of the program, she'd selected the intern who would be hired by the company as an assistant pharmacist.

During the two-month program, Noelle had cultivated and developed a camaraderie with the students. She was pleased the companionship hadn't ended when Eamon Taylor was given the job. Noelle had worried the remaining cohort would be standoffish toward her because of her decision, but they understood that only one of them could get the position.

Her confidence returning, Noelle began at the point where she'd trailed off and regained her composure quickly as she segued into her next talking point.

After the class ended, several of the students approached her to ask a few follow-up questions related to the lecture she'd given. Noelle was happy to provide additional insight and offer suggestions for further independent research on the topic.

As the students left the lecture hall, Noelle turned to the lectern and began gathering her note cards.

"Well, well, well, if it isn't the bitch who ruined my life," said

Helen, her voice slightly slurred and laced with spite.

Bristling at the familiar brassy tone, Noelle braced herself for the verbal attack and turned.

Helen Farber rose unsteadily from her seat and made her way down the steps and toward the lecture stage. Dressed in an orange Chanel suit which had seen much better days, Helen looked well beyond her forty years. Stage-like make-up couldn't hide the lines around her bleary eyes and pinched mouth.

"Good afternoon, Helen," said Noelle, deciding to stay calm and be cordial. "How are you?"

"How am I? Did you really just ask me, how am I?" Helen scoffed, her nasty smirk turning to an angry scowl. "Bitch, how do you think I am? I am working in a dead end job where I'm underutilized and overqualified. My life is destroyed, and it's your damn fault."

"Your life is not destroyed," Noelle said. "You can turn things around if you just get some help."

"I don't need your disingenuous motivational platitudes," Helen said, the furor between her painted eyebrows deepening. "You think I want advice from the bitch who stole my job."

"I didn't steal your job," Noelle said.

"You got me fired because you—"

"You got yourself fired," Noelle said, fighting to remain calm. "You weren't thinking about our customers, or—"

"I was going through a difficult time, okay?" Helen said, defensive, taking another step toward Noelle. "I thought you understood that because I thought we were friends, but instead you ratted on me."

Noelle stepped back. "I had to make sure that our customers weren't put in danger by your actions."

"You don't give a damn about our customers," said Helen. "You try to pretend that you're so kind and compassionate and caring, but I know the truth about you."

Noelle went rigid, panicked by Helen's claim.

"You're a con artist," Helen said, sneering. "People don't know who you really are, but—"

"People don't know the truth about you, either," said Noelle. "If they did, there is no way they would trust you to work around all these chemical substances."

"You back-stabbing bitch!" Helen said. "You may have it all together right now but one day your whole world is going to fall apart right before your eyes, and there won't be anything you can do to stop it."

"Are you drunk?" Noelle asked. "Or high?"

Helen gave a derisive snort and then said, "Here's what you need to remember, Noelle: Karma is a bitch ... and so am I."

Chapter Two

Karma is a bitch, and so am I …

Truer words were never spoken, thought Noelle as she exited the Pharmacy building and walked along a hibiscus lined path toward the university quad.

Helen was a bitch, but Noelle could be a bitch, too. She could be worse than a bitch, but she wouldn't give in to any hostile instincts. Noelle had promised herself she would never again "go all Handweg ho" on someone, no matter how bad they pissed her off.

Going "Handweg ho"— the pejorative expression assigned to young girls from Handweg Gardens—was no longer an option for her. Even though she was female and from the unofficial wrong side of the island, where tourists were warned never to tread, even in the daytime, she refused to be aggressive and confrontational at the drop of a hat for the slightest infraction, real or imagined.

Fifteen years ago, Noelle had decided she would no longer be defined by derogative generalizations based upon geographic location.

When she'd left St. Killian for a better life in America, she resolved to put her turbulent past behind her. After landing in Washington D.C. and moving in with her uncle, she began to change her narrative, to decide how she wanted others to perceive her.

The first step in her reinvention was changing her outward appearance. She ditched the baggy layers of clothing and dreadlocks and adopted the "girly-glam" feminine look of her cousins. She straightened her hair, learned how to apply her make-up, and patterned her style after the latest trends in Vogue magazine. Quickly, Noelle thrived in an atmosphere where she was encouraged and expected to succeed. She finished high school at the top of her class and went on to the University of North Carolina-Chapel Hill, where she studied at the Eshelman School of Pharmacy, ranked #1 in the United States.

The second step hadn't been as easy as sporting a new look. Sometimes Noelle wasn't sure she'd completely mastered reinventing her mindset. Reinvention meant more than adopting a glamorous persona. She'd had to learn how to think differently, how to solve her problems without threats or violence. Still, she'd struggled to walk away from conflict when everything within her wanted to "go all Handweg Ho" on whoever tried to start beef with her.

Noelle continued down the path, checking her watch. A few minutes after four-thirty. Enough time to stop at the market before she picked up her boys from her mother's house. Natalie Chartres, Noelle's mother, had recently declared herself the world's best granny, but Noelle knew it was because her boys, three-year-old Ethan and ten-month-old Evan, were the world's most perfect little munchkins.

As she reflected on her blessings, Noelle knew she shouldn't let Helen Farber get to her. The woman was depressed and damn near destitute, both financially and spiritually, following the disastrous mistakes which had derailed her career. Once on the fast track to a district management position with the Palmchat Pharmacy Company, Helen had squandered her opportunities when she'd become addicted to prescription pain medication.

After a debilitating back injury, Helen began to rely on the pills, continuing to take them even after she'd recovered. When she could no longer find a doctor to provide her with a prescription for the powerful medication, Helen began stealing drugs from the pharmacy.

When a customer had a pain medication prescription, Helen would fill the prescription with sugar pills and steal the pain pills she should have given to the customer. After several customer complaints, Noelle became suspicious and alerted the head of security at the company. The security department conducted an internal investigation and devised a sting to trap Helen.

After falling for the bait, Helen was terminated and her pharmacy license suspended indefinitely.

As she hurried down the path, Noelle took in her surroundings, hoping the beautiful campus, with its swaying palm trees and breathtaking views of the Caribbean sea, would take her mind off Helen's vicious verbal assault.

Salty breezes and abundant sunshine couldn't distract Noelle from the truth of Helen's tirade.

Helen was right about her. Noelle often felt like a con woman, fooling those around her. Since returning to St. Killian five years ago, Noelle had cleverly and craftily become the woman she'd always desired to be—the wife and mother with a great career. She'd taken great pains to make sure her past didn't come back to haunt her, which meant there were certain places she couldn't go and certain people she couldn't associate with, and—

Her cell phone chimed, and she stepped off the path to dig it from her purse.

Probably Beanie, she guessed, smiling as she thought about her better half, the man she'd vowed to love forever for better or for worse.

Her eternal Valentine, Roland "Beanie" Bean, was a reporter at the Palmchat Gazette. They'd met when Beanie was at his absolute worst—suffering from a horrible shellfish allergy.

Stumbling into the pharmacy late one night, he was half-blind from a swollen face and red, watery eyes. Noelle had just started working at the pharmacy the previous week, and his monstrous appearance almost made her forget her rigorous training. To make matters worse, Beanie's throat was so sore he couldn't talk. With horrible penmanship on both their parts, they'd been forced to communicate via text message. That was how he'd gotten her phone number.

A few days later, he'd texted her to thank her and to ask her out on a date. Remembering the bloated, miserable man, she'd been reluctant, but despite his terrible predicament, she'd seen a spark of interest and intelligence in those watery eyes. With no plans for the evening, she'd agreed to meet him at Dizzy Jenny's, a popular beachside restaurant. Noelle was glad she'd given him a chance. When he wasn't suffering from a food allergy, Beanie was quite tall, dark, and handsome.

Roland Bean was more attractive and appealing than the type of guys she'd once hooked up with.

Noelle glanced at her cell phone. A chill of dread passed through her. She stared at the text message, wishing she didn't recognize the anonymous number.

She knew exactly who was calling her—Grady Palmer, a nuisance from her past, an annoyance she couldn't associate with anymore. She couldn't avoid dealing with Grady. Very soon, Noelle would have to make some decisions about Grady and get him out of her life before—

Your whole world is going to fall apart right before your eyes, and there won't be anything you can do to stop it. Helen was wrong about that. Nothing was going to destroy what Noelle had with Beanie and her boys. She would fight with every fiber of her being to protect the beautiful life she'd made with her husband and children.

Determined to enjoy the beauty of the campus, Noelle walked leisurely yet with purpose. Although she was a proud Tarheel, she thought it might have been nice to further her education in paradise.

Who was she trying to fool, though? Certainly not herself. As she stepped onto the walkway which led to the faculty parking lot, Noelle knew that if she hadn't escaped St. Killian, she wouldn't have landed at the university.

She would have ended up in jail.

Or, more likely, dead.

Chapter Three

Pay what u owe mofo

Despite the warmth of the afternoon, Eamon Taylor felt an icy chill pass through him. *Pay what u owe mofo.* He knew exactly what would happen if he didn't pay the debt. With trembling fingers, Eamon deleted the text. It wasn't the first warning, and it wouldn't be the last.

If he didn't find a way to come up with the money, he would be killed.

"Eamon! Over here!" A chorus of excited voices to his left stole Eamon's attention from the threatening text message. Turning in the direction of the group calling to him, Eamon saw several acquaintances sitting at a table between two Sego palms.

Eamon pushed his phone into the front pocket of his jeans and started across the lawn, thankful for the distraction. At the picnic table, a rowdy, high-spirited debate raged between Tina Chen-Soo, Kevin Cook, Jimmy Quible, Sarah Linde, and Matt Delaney.

Taking a seat in the space between Tina and Matt, Eamon tried to focus on the conversation. They were talking about their job prospects. Specifically, the lack of job opportunities. Kevin, especially, was bitching more than he was bellyaching.

"What you have to realize," said Kevin, "is that the most qualified person doesn't always get the job."

"That's not true," disputed Tina.

"If you're good at what you do you'll get a job." Sarah rubbed Kevin's arm, an intimate gesture suggestive of a closer relationship, but Eamon caught the longing glance Sarah gave him—which he ignored. The extra-long looks had become more frequent recently, since their last hook-up two weeks ago. Eamon had rebuffed her persistent and aggressive advances, hoping she would take the hint and leave him the hell alone.

"Cream rises to the top," said Jimmy Quible, who sat on top of the table with his feet dangling.

"You know what else rises to the top?" asked Kevin, glancing at Eamon. "Scum."

A chorus of dispute erupted against Kevin, who was accused of having sour grapes and being unnecessarily negative and pessimistic.

"You guys know I'm right," Kevin said. "I mean, look at what happened with the Palmchat Pharmacy job. The smartest person didn't get it, and that doesn't really seem fair."

Eamon glared at Kevin. He was getting damn sick and tired of Kevin's sarcastic barbs, insinuating that Eamon hadn't deserved the Palmchat Pharmacy job. If Kevin made one more bullshit comment about his lack of intelligence or ability, Eamon was going to rip the whiny little bitch a new one.

"Well, maybe it's not fair but since you aren't the smartest intern," said Tina, with a smirk, "you weren't going to get the job anyway."

Tina's snappy, sassy comeback elicited laughter and clapping. Even Kevin had a self-effacing grin, knowing he'd been properly put in his place.

As the laughter died down, Sarah said, "Well, it's like Dr. Bean told us. We're all more than capable of being excellent pharmacists."

"Fuck her motivational bullshit," Kevin griped. "I almost hurled when she said, 'I wish I could have hired all of you.' Yeah, right ..."

"It's not bullshit, dude," said Jimmy. "Plus, she's gonna give us recommendations."

Kevin scoffed. "Like a recommendation from some island twat is going to do me a damn bit of good."

"Dr. Bean is not an island twat," said Eamon, itching to lunge across the table, put his hands around Kevin's scrawny neck, and choke the shit out of him. An aggressive reaction would only give Kevin more ammunition against him, though. Eamon didn't want to be stereotyped as just another Handweg hood.

"You shouldn't say that, Kevin." Sarah frowned as she scooted away from him. "It's rude and misogynistic and sexist."

"Look, we all knew there was only one position," said Matt. "Only one person was going to get it."

Nodding, Tina said, "We should just be happy for the opportunity that Palmchat Pharmacy provided us."

"Eamon is the only one who got an opportunity to get the job," Kevin said, his tone caustic. "The rest of us never had a chance. We're not from Handweg Gardens."

"What does me being from Handweg Gardens have to do with me getting the job?" Eamon demanded.

"You know exactly what it means," Kevin said. "You island people stick together and help each other, whether you deserve it, or not."

"Fuck you, Kevin." Eamon stood and walked away from the table. Ignoring the calls to return, he crossed the Palm-dotted quad and headed to the library. Kevin Cook deserved a punch in the throat but walking away had been the best thing to do. Guys like Kevin ultimately weren't worth the bruised knuckles. Eamon had decided long ago he wouldn't solve his problems with his fists. People expected Handweg guys to be aggressive and violent, but he'd vowed not to live up to negative stereotypes.

As he stepped onto the path leading toward the library, someone called his name. Recognizing the irritating high-pitched tone, Eamon hurried into the library, deciding to pretend he hadn't heard the voice behind him. Walking past the information counter, he made a right and headed toward the bookshelves.

Hoping he could navigate through the maze of shelves and make it upstairs to a private study room without being cornered, Eamon made another right, trying to zig-zag his way back to the main lobby where he would catch an elevator, but he accidentally made a left and was caught.

"Didn't you hear me?" Sarah Linde's lowered voice held traces of annoyance.

Eamon shook his head. "No, I—"

"Fucking liar," Sarah said.

Eamon sighed. "Look—"

"Why have you been ignoring me?"

"Sarah—"

"I miss you," she said, her voice still a whisper but childishly sexy now as she stepped closer to him. "I miss you inside me. It's all I can think about."

Laughing softly, he shook his head and sighed.

"Why are you laughing?" She glared at him. "You think it's funny that I'm addicted to you? Does it amuse you to know that I can't stop thinking about when we were together?"

"It was a mistake," Eamon said.

Sarah frowned. "What?"

"When we hooked-up," he said, switching his backpack from his left shoulder to his right. "We were drunk and high."

"It was not a mistake. How can you say that?" she asked, lower lip quivering. "What we shared that night was special. Cosmic. Mystical. Supernatural. It was—"

Exhaling, he said, "It was the ecstasy we took before we fucked, okay?"

Sarah scowled. "How can you be so cruel and crude? That night was beautiful and pure. I've never felt that way before."

Eamon scoffed. "I doubt that."

Glowering at him, she said, "I am not some hit it and forget it, girl, okay? We did not have a casual hook-up. It meant something. I know you know that. I know you want me just as much as I want you."

"Listen, I gotta go, but maybe I'll call you," Eamon said, maneuvering around her.

Nails stabbed into his arm, piercing the skin.

Wincing, Eamon turned and yanked his arm from her death grip. "What the hell is your problem?"

"Don't you dare try to dismiss me," she warned. "I won't be ignored. You break my heart, and I swear, I will rip yours right out of your chest."

Blue eyes hard, nostrils flaring, Sarah shoulder-checked him as she stomped away.

Watching her leave, Eamon touched the welts she'd left on his skin.

"Fucking psycho bitch," he muttered under his breath as he shook his head.

Sarah Linde was crazy as hell. Was she out of her mind? They hadn't shared any magical, cosmic sex. What Eamon remembered was mediocre, at best. Just two horny people using each other to get off. Nothing special or supernatural about it.

Walking slowly through the bookshelves, Eamon remembered Kevin's warning about Sarah's strange possessive attachment. "She's a quick, easy fuck," Kevin had told him. "She's down for whatever, but be careful because she likes to fall in love."

Slightly apprehensive, Eamon glanced at the scratches on his arm, the mark of Sarah's rage. As much as he wanted to dismiss her threat as the ranting of a spurned lover, Eamon wondered if maybe he shouldn't shrug off Sarah's threat.

He wondered if Sarah might be dangerous.

Chapter Four

Heading back into his bedroom with a steaming mug of coffee, Eamon Taylor went to the desk in the corner of the room, sat down and started up his computer.

After a few hesitant sips of the strong, percolated brew, he opened his email.

Before he could read the first message, his phone vibrated. Eamon felt a fluttering of panic swirling through his veins as he checked the text message. Another warning, this one even more intimidating and incendiary than the last few he'd received over the past month.

U must want 2 die. ignore me at ur own risk

Eamon ran a hand down the back of his close-cropped faux hawk. He wasn't sure if he should go to the cops ... or handle the situation himself. He knew he could. Eamon had been born and raised in Handweg Gardens. Though he'd never succumbed to island gang life, he was sure he could hold his own against a threat.

Or, maybe not.

Sighing, he sent a response.

not ignoring u just need more time. will b n touch soon.

Hoping he'd bought himself some time, Eamon focused on his Inbox. He stared at the first email and frowned. Another strange email full of intimidating and incendiary language. This one was even more disturbing than the last email.

The first email had been sent to Eamon a month ago, during his first week on his new job at the Palmchat Pharmacy. Eamon hadn't taken it seriously. He'd figured it was a joke. Kevin or Matt or Tina trying to punk him. Kevin Cook, especially, was into playing stupid pranks. The PharmD he'd earned had done little to mature Kevin. He was still the same sophomoric asshole Eamon had met four years ago.

The email had been more annoying than funny. Eamon had deleted it, not giving it another thought.

Until he'd received the second email the following week. The message had been similar to the message in the first email, weird, confusing and slightly terrorizing. The last lines of the email had mirrored the last line of the first email: *Don't ignore me, Eamon. Or, I will destroy your life.*

A third email had come last week, similar to the first two, the tone lurid and dangerous. The last line read: *Ignoring me is a mistake. I can make your life a living hell.*

He stared at the email he'd just opened. The last line was similar to the last line of the previous emails: *Keep ignoring me, and I will ruin you.*

Eamon didn't understand. What the hell was going on? Why was this happening? Why send these emails to him? Why try to force him to do something he didn't want to do? The emails featured the same proposition. A proposal he couldn't accept.

You're the only one who can do this, Eamon. I need to know what your answer will be.

Focusing on the sender's email address, Eamon wondered if maybe he could use the emails to his advantage. He knew the sender. That person had a lot to lose if anyone found out about the emails. Eamon had a lot to gain if he exposed the strange, terrorizing messages.

The email messages were disturbing, but Eamon didn't think his life was going to become a living hell or be ruined. The threatening text messages had to be taken seriously, but the email messages were nothing to really be afraid of ...

Eamon took a few more sips of coffee.

The email messages weren't as scary as the letters from Sarah

Linde. She'd sent him a few bizarre manifestos about love and death and other bullshit he didn't understand. He'd shown the letters to Kevin and Matt, and they'd all had a good laugh.

Finishing his coffee, Eamon stood. They said things came in threes, didn't they? Heading into the shower, he realized that he was currently dealing with three different threats. One was comical, one was as serious as a stroke, and the other just might save his ass ...

Chapter Five

"Will you be okay if I head out a bit early?"

Startled by the voice behind him, too familiar and much too close, Eamon Taylor took a quick breath. Struggling to compose himself, he prayed to maintain a calm demeanor as he turned to face Dr. Noelle Bean, his boss at Palmchat Pharmacy.

"Um, no," Eamon said, trying not to stammer. "I mean, yeah, I'll be fine. We're slow today anyway."

Eamon had serviced his last client about a half hour ago, an older grandmotherly type who'd wanted a recommendation to approve her memory. Should she take St. John's Wort or Coenzyme Q10? Eamon had painstakingly explained the differences between the supplements, taking care to answer any and all questions.

Ultimately, the elderly woman had decided not to buy anything, but she'd left the pill bottles on the counter. Eamon had instructed the pharmacy tech on duty to return them to aisle three, where the supplements were stocked. The tech claimed to be swamped with paperwork. A dubious claim, one the tech often relied on when she didn't want to take orders from him, Eamon had noticed.

The dearth of customers, which was unusual for a Tuesday afternoon, prompted him to aisle three, where he'd been restocking the supplements when Dr. Bean had sneaked up behind him.

"Are you sure it's okay?" Dr. Bean asked. Standing across the aisle, she was polished and professional in her white lab coat with her hair pulled back in a bun and reading glasses perched on her nose. "I don't want to leave you hanging."

"I'm sure," Eamon said. "It's fine."

Dr. Bean smiled. Eamon tried to return the smile, but he struggled to force the corners of his mouth to lift. He couldn't believe how graceful and considerate she seemed. He couldn't believe that her kindness and compassion was just a façade.

"I hate to skip out, but ..." Dr. Bean went on, explaining why she wanted to leave early, but Eamon wasn't listening. Fighting a nagging sense of disappointment and discouragement, he couldn't help feeling like an idiot for believing Dr. Bean had his best interests at heart.

During the internship, she'd been nice to him, motivating and helpful, always willing to answer any questions he had and eager to give advice.

When he'd started at the pharmacy, Eamon had been eager to work with her.

As the lead pharmacist of the St. Killian location, Dr. Bean was practiced and experienced, the model of proficient efficiency. Her knowledge of pharmaceutical sciences was astounding, and she was a gifted communicator, adept at clearly imparting what she knew.

During his first week, as they'd worked side by side, Eamon had thought he and Dr. Bean might become more than just co-workers or colleagues ...

Now, he couldn't stand the sight of the bitch.

"So, I'm off tomorrow," said Dr. Bean. "But, I'll see you on Thursday."

Eamon nodded, wishing she would just leave already.

"Oh, and I wanted to tell you," she said, giving him another fake smile. "I think you're doing a great job. I'm glad I chose you for the position."

Eamon's heart slammed as Dr. Bean walked away from him, striding down the aisle and around the corner, out of his view.

Lying whore, Eamon thought, his chest tightening. Did Dr. Noelle Bean really think she could fuck with him and get away with it?

Well, the bitch would do well to think again ...

Chapter Six

"Babe, what happened to your hand?" Beanie asked. "You cut yourself?"

"What?" Noelle slipped her hand from Beanie's strong, gentle grasp.

Moments ago, her husband had been about to kiss the inside of her palm, a move specifically designed to get her all hot and bothered.

He'd kissed her palm for the first time five years ago, at the end of their first date. When his lips touched her skin, the sensation had twirled and fluttered directly to her most intimate places. Despite the lust flooding her body, Noelle had known she'd found her soul mate.

Noelle had been eagerly anticipating the kiss, even though it always made her so horny, all she could think about was ripping her husband's clothes off, something she couldn't do at the moment.

She and Beanie were at Dizzy Jenny's, three courses into their monthly decadent date night, a tradition they'd started after the birth of Ethan, their three-year-old. Becoming a mother had been a dream come true, but she hadn't wanted to neglect her husband's needs or her own. Date night had been a way to make sure they continued to make love like they were newlyweds on their honeymoon.

Glancing at the long, thin scratch beneath her right knuckle trailing in a jagged line to her wrist, Noelle shrugged. "I cut myself when I was planting those rose bushes yesterday."

Grabbing her hand again, Beanie made a sympathetic noise as he kissed the scar that had formed.

"I can't remember if it was a thorn," she said, "or that damn shovel. Still can't believe somebody stole it."

Beanie released her hand to pick up his wine glass. "Whoever took the shovel did you a favor."

"Roland," scolded Noelle, picking up her glass of chardonnay. "How can you say that?"

"That shovel was raggedy, Elle," he said, using the pet name he sometimes called her. "The blade was bent, and one of the foot rests was dented."

"I got a good deal on that shovel," said Noelle. "I had to haggle with Mr. Ross for—"

"An hour before he caved and let you have it for half off," Beanie said, playfully finishing the story she'd proudly recounted when she purchased the shovel two weeks ago.

"Just pisses me off that someone took it because I barely got to use it."

"Babe, I'll buy you a new shovel."

Noelle smiled and then took another sip of wine. She had the most wonderful husband in the world. Beanie was her hero, always trying to make everything better and keep her happy. He was so different from the kind of guy she figured she'd end up with—a man who didn't care about her feelings or her needs. When she was a teenager before she'd left St. Killian, she'd always been involved with violent misogynists, men who were verbally, and sometimes physically, abusive.

She'd assumed she would be with a degenerate with homicidal tendencies—a man like her father.

"What about some dessert?" Beanie tossed his napkin onto his plate, covering the few remnants of the coq au vin he'd ordered.

Noelle nodded. "First, I want to call Sarah and see how the boys are doing."

Sarah Linde, one of the students from the Palmchat Pharmacy Internship program, had become close to Noelle during the two months when they were mentor/mentee. Sarah's mother was the director of an early childhood development center, and the young woman had spent her teen years assisting teachers who cared for toddlers. When Noelle's mother was unable to care for the boys, she trusted Sarah to watch Ethan and Evan.

"Helicopter mom," said Beanie, teasing. "The boys are just fine, Elle."

Noelle said, "I know, but ..."

"But, let's order dessert," Beanie suggested. "What about the strawberry shortcake?"

"Sounds good," said Noelle as she pushed back from the table and stood.

"Where are you going?"

"I've been drinking wine all evening," she said, grabbing her purse from the back of the chair.

"Give me your phone," Beanie said, smiling at her.

With a resigned sigh, Noelle opened her purse, took out her phone and tossed it at him. Giving Beanie what she hoped was a grumpy look, Noelle turned, leaving him laughing at her. He knew her too well, she thought as she headed to the ladies room.

It was a lovely night, with a warm breeze and stars twinkling overhead in an expansive indigo sky. The perfect night for a romantic dinner with the man of her dreams. Clinking glasses and whispered conversations floated through the air as Noelle navigated the tables in the beachfront dining area. She passed the U-shaped bar and strode to the alcove where the restrooms were located, near the back of the restaurant, close to the bustling kitchen.

In the ladies room, Noelle went into a stall, locked the door and leaned against it. She felt a bit bereft, and slightly adrift, without a phone to check on her boys. Beanie was right, though. The boys were okay. She trusted Sarah. If an issue came up, the young woman had strict instructions to call Noelle immediately.

Still, when she wasn't with the boys, she did get a bit obsessive and spastic, Noelle supposed. Beanie didn't understand. He couldn't because he hadn't carried the boys in his womb. She had been responsible for the boys in a way he never had. Together, they had created life, but she'd had to sustain that life with her own life. Ethan and Evan had depended upon her for their very existence. Sometimes, she probably was a little too overprotective, but it was only because she finally had something important and precious to love and protect. She never thought she would have a family of her own. Now that Beanie and the boys were her world, she was desperate to make sure nothing bad happened. She couldn't lose what she knew she didn't deserve.

Exiting the stall, Noelle washed her hands at one of the sinks. Checking her appearance in the long, wide mirror above the counter, she studied the high cheek bones and full lips, the sculpted face and smooth skin the color of West Indian mahogany, and the long column of straight black hair. Beanie always told her she was the prettiest girl in the Palmchat Islands, but Noelle didn't always agree with his opinion. She knew she was attractive, but sometimes when she looked in the mirror, she didn't see the pretty, polished pharmacist.

Often she saw the girl she'd once been staring back at her—fifteen-year-old Noelle "Nobody" Chartres with the sneer and the scowl, hiding behind the tough exterior.

Sometimes, Noelle wondered if she was still Nobody. Maybe the reinvention was just a façade. A mask she wore to fool people. *I know the truth about you.* Noelle pushed Helen Farber's words from her mind. Her past wasn't the only truth about her.

The truth was who she'd become, the woman she was right now—wife, mother, pharmacist.

Moments later, as she walked out of the restroom, Noelle collided with a waitress and dropped her purse.

"Oh, I'm sorry!" The waitress gave her a pained look of frustration and embarrassment. "I'm so dumb! I need to watch where I'm going!"

"No, it's okay," Noelle said, figuring the girl was hurrying to take a quick bathroom break.

"Sorry," the waitress continued her profuse apologies as she headed into the ladies room. Noelle shook her head, remembering her purse. Glancing down, she frowned.

Her purse was gone.

Heart slamming, she scanned the floor. Her confusion quickly turned to suspicion. Had the collision with the waitress been an accident? Or some distraction, designed to—

"Looking for this?"

The voice, low, deep and much too close to her ear, sent the chill of dread through her body. Determined to manage the fear and anger battling within her, Noelle turned.

She almost gasped but managed to keep her composure in the face of Grady Palmer's lewd smirk.

Noelle hadn't seen Grady in fifteen years, but time hadn't changed him. He didn't seem much older than the twenty-year-old bad boy who was known in Handweg as Psycho. When they used to hang out, and occasionally hook up, Grady had been known for his unpredictable mood swings. One minute he was seductive, the next sinister.

Noelle stepped back, glaring at the past she'd left behind and never wanted to visit again.

One reason Noelle had felt comfortable returning to St. Killian was because many of her old friends and enemies had left the island in the past fifteen years since she'd been gone. There were still a few enemies around, but fifteen years was a long time, and many of them had either forgotten about her or weren't interested in her transformation.

Handweg Gardens wasn't a place she could avoid since her mother still lived in the rough neighborhood. Nevertheless, there were certain people she didn't want to see again, people she couldn't face again, people who might try to force her back into her old life, the life she'd resolved to give up for good.

People like Grady Palmer.

"Give me my purse," she said, her tone calm and even. The urge to rely on old instincts she'd developed and honed in Handweg Gardens was strong, but she resisted. Using violence to solve her problems wasn't an option anymore.

Grady held out the purse to her.

"What the hell do you want?" She snatched the purse from him, glancing around, fearful and furtive. "Did you follow me here?"

"Let's go have a seat," he said, clutching her elbow, practically shoving her toward the divan.

"Get your hands off me," she whispered through clenched teeth.

"Careful, Mrs. Bean," said Grady, pulling her down with him as he took a seat. "Don't want to make a scene. Don't want nobody to know that beneath all the fancy exterior, you're still just a Handweg Ho."

Noelle yanked her arm away from him.

"You think because you left the island and went to some expensive private school and a fancy college that you've changed. You think you're somebody now?" Grady shook his head in amazement. "You think you're different now because you found some punk to put a ring on it?"

"My husband is not a punk," she said. "He's a better man than you will ever be."

"And there she is," said Grady, smiling as though he'd made some startling discovery. "The Handweg ho. I knew she was still there. You can try to pretend she doesn't exist but we both know the truth. You may look like some uppity educated bitch, but you're still the girl who used to—"

"What the hell do you want?" She cut him off, not wanting to be reminded of the things she'd done.

"You know what I want."

"And I'm not going to do it," she said. "I won't."

"You're not really in a position to tell me what you're not going to do."

"You're not really in a position to make me do a damn thing," she snapped.

"I'm in a position to make your life hell, bitch," Grady said, grabbing her arm, digging his fingers into her flesh as he leaned toward her. "I'm in a position to hurt people that you care about."

Trembling, Noelle cut her gaze toward him, trying to ignore the horror of his words.

"You and I go way back," Grady said. "You know what I'm capable of and you know I don't make empty threats."

"You don't understand," Noelle said. "I can't do what you want."

"I think you can and you will," he said. "Because you know what will happen if you don't."

"You try to hurt my family," she said, the anger taking over, "and I will kill you."

Scoffing, Grady gave a wry smile as he stood. "I knew you hadn't changed."

Shamed by the veracity of his judgment, Noelle looked away, disturbed by how quickly she'd reverted to her old way of reacting to confrontation.

"I trust you understand what's at risk, Mrs. Bean," he said. "So, I'll be in touch. Don't ignore my texts."

As Grady walked away, Noelle let out the breath she wasn't aware she'd been holding. Tears threatened, but she blinked and pressed a finger beneath her eyes. She didn't need Grady Palmer to tell her what was at risk. Everything was at risk. Her entire life. Her husband. Her children. Her career. Her freedom, most of all.

Noelle stood, taking another breath to get her bearings. Grady was wrong. She had changed. She wasn't a Handweg Ho anymore, but she was still a fighter. She wasn't about to let a psychotic bastard destroy everything she loved most in the world.

If Grady Palmer went after her family, Noelle would kill him.

Chapter Seven

Roland "Beanie" Bean read the message he'd just received from Sarah Linde.

Beautiful boys sleeping peacefully, dreaming sweetly!

After Noelle had left to go to the bathroom, Beanie had used her phone to text the babysitter and make sure the boys were okay. When she returned, he would show her the text, which would ease her mind.

Beanie teased Elle about being a helicopter mom, but he hovered over their boys as much as she did. He just wasn't so obvious about it. Worrying was part of parenting, he'd learned. When Noelle had told him she was pregnant with Ethan, he had been ecstatic but apprehensive also. Before he knew if he and Noelle were having a boy or a girl, Beanie began questioning himself and his abilities. Was he ready to be a father? Who was ever ready to be responsible for the nurturing and care of another life? Of course, he wasn't ready, but he was eager and excited and more than sure that he and Noelle were capable of being good shepherds and positive influences. They would raise compassionate, intelligent, empathetic young boys who would have integrity, be strong in their convictions and strive to help others and do no harm.

What he worried most about was providing for his children. He'd grown up loved and well-rounded, with parents who had honest intentions and a strong work ethic. What they didn't have was tons of money. He knew he wouldn't have wealth and privilege to offer his children, but he could give them a strong sense of purpose and the spirit of enterprise and industry he'd been exposed to, which could take them far in life if applied correctly.

Nevertheless, Beanie wondered if he hadn't gone far enough in life for his kids. He wanted to give them the best life possible. At times, he doubted his choice of profession, which had been chosen when he was young and wasn't thinking about any future responsibilities.

Now, he thought maybe he should have been a doctor or a lawyer. Maybe he should have chosen a profession which would have guaranteed him a generous salary with no worries about his employment outlook, which was sometimes unstable, at best.

Last year, when Burt Bronson bought the Palmchat Gazette, Beanie feared he would lose his job.

The publishing legend was known for buying small-market publications and for his gruff demeanor, which was sometimes overbearing and intimidating. Besides his critical editorial demands, Bronson was notorious for brutally cutting expenses through workforce reductions.

Bronson had spared most of the staff reporters to Beanie's immense relief. Still, once the threat of unemployment no longer consumed his mind, Beanie began to realize that the paper wasn't offering him any real career advancement.

With Bronson in charge, Beanie had expected to write stories that made a difference to the people of St. Killian. He'd wanted to move past just reporting the facts about crime in Handweg Gardens. He wanted to craft in-depth analysis pieces about the systemic reasons for the crime in Handweg. Many of the *Palmchat Gazette* headlines read, BODY FOUND DEAD IN HANDWEG GARDENS. There was more to those stories than just the corpse and the cops giving their standard "no comment" response. There was a victim who deserved a voice and a suspect who had to be understood so that other crimes could be prevented.

Beanie had spoken to Bronson about his ideas, and the man had seemed amenable.

So, why was he still monitoring the police scanner? Well, he couldn't really blame Bronson. The man had recently suffered a major heart attack, and his vision for the Palmchat Gazette was on hold.

While Bronson recuperated, his son, Leo, was in charge.

Beanie had mixed feelings about working for a guy who obviously would have rather been chasing crazy African warlords instead of babysitting a group of island reporters. Noelle had encouraged him to give Leo Bronson a chance, and he'd agreed. Secretly, Beanie thought he might be jealous of Burt's cavalier son. Maybe his aversion to working for Leo was more about his own stalled and stymied career.

More than a year ago, Beanie had hoped to give his career a shot it the arm by taking over the crime beat, but when Vivian Thomas was hired, she was a natural for the position. Having spent years in Africa exposing the high crimes and atrocities of brutal dictators, Vivian brought a confident experience to the paper which was reflected in her stellar investigations.

Sometimes Beanie felt like a great reporter without a great story.

"Everything okay, Mr. Bean?" The waiter asked.

Beanie nodded. "Everything is great. The Coq au vine was especially good."

He and the waiter chatted a bit more, and then Beanie put in the strawberry shortcake order. As the waiter drifted to another table, he wondered, where was his wife? From their table near the beach, Beanie had a direct view of the restroom alcove at the back of the restaurant, but another waiter standing at a table a few feet away blocked his line of sight.

When the waiter stepped away from the table, Beanie stared directly across the restaurant.

He frowned, a fissure of apprehension passing through him.

Normally when Beanie saw something suspicious, he went into journalist mode, looking for the who, what, when, where, why, or how. But, was he staring at something suspicious? Beanie hoped not. He didn't want to be suspicious of what he saw. He wanted to evaluate the facts he knew so far, but he found it impossible to process the situation like he would a news story.

The only way he could deal with the situation was as a husband who was confused, trying to manage the emotions churning within him as he wondered what the hell was happening.

Why was Noelle sitting much too close to another man on the couch in the restroom alcove?

Chapter Eight

"Who was that guy you were talking to at the restaurant?" Beanie asked.

Shocked, Noelle took a breath and tried not to panic.

Beanie had seen her talking to Grady Palmer. Filled with fear and frustration, she tried to think of an answer to give Beanie, something believable that would put his mind at ease.

"Are you taking the coastal highway?" Noelle asked, straining against the seatbelt as she peered through the front windshield. "Because it would be quicker if you took—"

"Are you avoiding my question?"

Picking up on the hint of irritation in his tone, Noelle fought the urge to scream and curse. She had to diffuse the situation before it got out of control. She didn't want to lie to her husband. When they'd made their vows before God and their family, they'd promised to forsake all others, but she couldn't tell Beanie about Grady Palmer.

Her husband could never know the truth about her past.

As far as Beanie was concerned, she was a Handweg Gardens success story.

"Noelle ..." Beanie prompted, a hint of some other emotion in his voice. Jealousy? Why? Beanie couldn't be jealous, could he? Didn't he realize by now that there was no other man she would ever want but him? Had Beanie seen her talking to Grady and thought she was interested in that savage son of a bitch? God, she hoped not. She prayed Beanie didn't think she would ever cheat on him.

"Oh, you mean the guy I was talking to by the restrooms?" Noelle asked, trying to project a tone somewhere between confusion and realization.

"Yeah, that guy," said Beanie.

"One of my customers who came in to have a prescription filled today," Noelle said, hating the lies she had no choice but to tell. "As soon as he recognized me, he had a hundred questions about his medication. I should have told him you were waiting. I'm sorry."

"It's okay," Beanie said, with a trace of relief. "I know how much you care about your customers."

Disgusted by her dishonesty, Noelle said nothing. She was thankful for the dark interior of their SUV and the minimal street lights on the stretch of road leading back to their house in Oyster Farm Estates, a modest neighborhood of single story Colonial houses on generous plots of land. At least Beanie couldn't see her face, which she was sure reflected the guilt coursing through her veins.

Beanie chuckled softly, steering the SUV around a slight curve in the road.

"Why did you laugh?" Noelle stared at his silhouette profile.

"Just thinking about what I originally thought when I saw you and the guy talking."

Pulse racing, she asked, "What did you think?"

Beanie said nothing.

Noelle fought panic as the silence between them lengthened. "You didn't think I was meeting up with some secret lover, or something, did you?"

It was a risky question. She might be opening up a brand new can of worms, but she hoped the question would act as a segue to a different topic, a more salacious topic to steer her husband away from what he'd witnessed between her and Grady at Dizzy Jenny's.

Beanie exhaled and said, "I might have thought that."

"Well, you shouldn't have," Noelle said, determined to invoke a more amorous mood. "You're the only lover I want, and that's not a secret."

"Is that so?" Beanie asked, stopping the SUV at a red traffic light.

"Absolutely."

"Prove it," said Beanie, his tone enticingly teasing.

Noelle laughed out loud. "What?"

"You heard me," Beanie said, grabbing her left arm, placing her hand between his legs.

Through his pants, Noelle felt his erection, huge and stiff, and was instantly turned on, hot and wet just thinking about taking advantage of her handsome husband. Reaching over the console, she fiddled with the button on his slacks and pulled the zipper down.

Beanie slid an arm around her waist, pulled her onto his lap and positioned her between his legs. Sitting on the very edge of the seat, in the middle of his thighs, Noelle stared through the windshield at the road stretching before them.

"Grab the wheel," Beanie ordered.

Confused, Noelle stared at the steering wheel.

"The light is green," he said. "Take the wheel."

"Are you serious?" Noelle asked as she realized that the car was moving, but Beanie was no longer driving. He was busy grabbing the hem of her dress, pulling it up to her waist.

He struggled to pull her panties down past her hips. "I'm a little busy right now."

Heart pounding, Noelle put her left hand on '10' and her right hand at '2'.

"Raise up a bit," he said.

Using the wheel to steady herself, Noelle lifted up from the seat a few inches, half-standing as she gripped the wheel, trying to keep the car steady.

Beanie pushed the panties down to her knees. He slipped a finger inside of her, and then another one, hooking both fingers toward the front of her vagina, caressing that sensitive spot while his thumb moved in a slow, circle around her clit. A throbbing ache started to build, and involuntarily, Noelle moved her hips, rubbing against his thumb, hesitant at first, until the sensations begin to intensify. She moved faster, not quite in a frenzy but almost there as she felt the orgasm, surging, rushing forward from deep within her.

Gasping, Noelle clutched the steering wheel, closing her eyes.

The SUV veered to the left.

"Pay attention to the road, Mrs. Bean," Beanie instructed.

Shuddering, Noelle opened her eyes. She jerked the wheel to the right, trying to keep the SUV on the road while Beanie removed his fingers, grabbed her hips and lifted her higher.

"What are you doing?" she asked, trying to keep the wheel steady.

"Open your legs just a bit."

Her nipples hardened, and the warm, heavy ache between her legs increased as the feelings began to consume her.

The SUV glided off the road and down onto the shoulder, the chassis rocking slightly.

Beanie laughed and took the wheel again. Guiding the SUV toward a row of Seagrape trees, he parked the SUV and cut the engine. "I thought you were supposed to be keeping us on the road."

Noelle didn't reply, too engaged in frantically moving her hips back and forth, rubbing against his penis, practically seething in anticipation of the orgasm.

Beanie lifted her up again and then lowered her onto him, grasping her hips. Slowly, slowly, Noelle felt him sliding into her, stretching her. Moving her hips back and forth, up and down, in circles, Noelle leaned over the wheel as she set the rhythm, fast, slow, even slower, and then faster.

Clutching her hips, Beanie moved her up and down on his penis, forcing her to keep up with his breakneck pace before abruptly bringing things almost to a complete stop. As Noelle grabbed the steering wheel, he plunged deeper and harder. Soon, she felt a sweet, pulsating, electric implosion, deep within her. The convulsions continued, spiraling, surging through her like bombs exploding.

Collapsing back against Beanie, Noelle closed her eyes as the pulsating tremors slowly subsided.

Chapter Nine

Disgruntled and disgusted, Eamon Taylor glared at Kevin Cook, slouched on the couch, drinking his third Felipe beer, and Matt Delaney lounged in the recliner, nursing his second.

If Kevin and Matt weren't his classmates, Eamon probably wouldn't have had anything to do with them. He had nothing in common with the spoiled Americans, who felt they were entitled to whatever they wanted, when they wanted it, whether it belonged to them, or not.

Especially Kevin. He was the worst.

Matt actually wasn't so bad when Kevin wasn't around to influence him. Kevin, however, was an arrogant prick, pissed because he hadn't been accepted to a pharmacy school in the states. Despite St. Killian University's reputation as the "Caribbean Princeton," Kevin thought the university wasn't good enough and felt he was slumming. Often, Kevin made disparaging comments about the university, claiming he would have a hard time getting a good job with the school on his resume.

Lazy bastards, thought Eamon, sitting on the scarred surface of the old coffee table his aunt had given him. Kevin and Matt only stopped by when they were broke and had run out of beer. Tonight, though, he was glad they were here. He needed to talk to them.

After getting a Felipe beer from the refrigerator for himself, Eamon sat on the opposite end of the lumpy couch and explained his predicament.

The job at Palmchat Pharmacy had started out well, very promising. Eamon had been nervous the first week, but Dr. Bean and his other co-workers were genuinely nice and helpful. Excited to have him join the team, they seemed committed to making sure he did a good job, which, in turn, would help the pharmacy and its customers.

Eamon had been nervous, but eager to show Dr. Bean he was focused and capable of being an important asset to the company. There was a learning curve, of course, but Eamon had been a quick study. He was efficient, effective and productive, maintaining speed and accuracy. With the customers, some of whom were initially hesitant about a new pharmacist, he proved to be patient and understanding.

The second week mirrored the first week, with one exception.

On Friday of the second week, he received an email with a very suggestive message ...

You did well today ... I've love to find out how well you would do me

Eamon had deleted the email, thinking it was a dumb joke perpetrated by his classmates. Then another email showed up in his inbox the following week, similar to the first email but with an obvious threat.

You looked so good today. I couldn't stop thinking about how good we could be together. I want you so bad. When I'm with my husband, I wish he were you. I want to meet you somewhere so you can make all my fantasies come true. Let me know when we can meet. Don't ignore me, Eamon. Or, I will destroy your life.

Another email followed that same week with a slightly different threat after the proposition. *I can make your life a living hell.*

And then there was the latest email. *I need you to make me feel good. You're the only one who can do this, Eamon. I need to know what your answer will be. Keep ignoring me, and I will ruin you.*

Along with the threat, there had been an attachment. Against his better judgment, Eamon had opened it.

He wished he hadn't.

"Let me see the attachment," said Kevin, sitting his beer on the coffee table. Eamon stood, went into his bedroom and retrieved the folder where he kept copies of the emails. Back in the tiny living area, he tossed the offensive attachment to Kevin.

"Let me see it," said Matt, after Kevin started to smile and snicker.

"It's not funny," Eamon said, glaring at Kevin.

Still laughing, Kevin handed the color copy to Matt. "Dude, is that shit real? What the hell?"

"Yes, this shit is beyond real," Eamon said. "And I need to know what the hell to do about it."

"Bro, I hate to tell you, but this photo isn't real," said Matt, staring intently at the color photocopy of the email attachment. "You can tell it's been doctored. I won't even say Photoshopped because that would be an insult to the software. Very amateurish."

"I know the picture is fake." Eamon snatched the email from Matt. "That's not the point. The point is the message she's conveying."

"The message she's conveying is that she wants you to bone her." Kevin shrugged. "Doesn't seem like a problem to me."

"You don't think these emails are a problem?" Eamon stared at Kevin, pissed at his smug indifference. "Are you serious?"

Kevin shrugged again. "I'd do her. She's hot. Kind of Naomi Campbell-ish. A total MILF."

Matt snickered.

Eamon shook his head, confounded by Kevin's flippant obtuse attitude. "Did you really just say that?"

"Look, just do the bitch," Kevin said. "What do you have to lose?"

"His job," said Matt. "Maybe."

"All the more reason to give her what she wants," Kevin said. "The way I see it, you owe her a fuck."

Eamon was speechless for a few seconds. "Wait. Did you just say that I owe her?"

"Look, let's cut the shit, okay. She gave you a job you didn't deserve. A Handweg handout," Kevin said. "And now it's clear why you got the job. Because she wants a Handweg put out."

"I got the job because I was the most qualified," Eamon said, blood roaring through his head, pissed that Kevin was still so damn bitter about not getting the assistant pharmacist position.

"Yeah, but the most qualified at what?" Kevin scoffed, scowling. "Getting her off?"

"Son of a bitch ..." Eamon stood, anxious to slam his fist in the middle of Kevin's sunburned face.

"Guys, chill, okay ..." Matt jumped up and stepped in front of Eamon, his expression pained as his head whipped back and forth between Kevin and Eamon. "Don't come to blows over this, please."

Eamon turned away from Kevin, staring toward the kitchen. Matt was right. Wasn't worth it to beat Kevin's ass right now. The last thing he needed was an assault charge, which he was sure he'd get because Kevin's punk ass would press charges against him. Neither did he want to prove his Handweg relatives right. His cousins always accused him of thinking he was better than them, but they'd promised him that, one day, he'd be exposed for what he really was—just another island thug.

Sighing, Kevin ran his hand down the back of his sandy curls. "Look, if the emails really bother you, then just go to Human Resources. File a claim against the bitch. Get her fired."

Eamon took a deep breath, grabbed his beer from the coffee table and took a swig. "I thought about going to HR, but she's well respected in the company. She's a superstar. Everybody loves her. If I'm gonna bring a claim against her, I need solid proof."

Matt said, "The emails should be all the proof you need."

"Maybe not," Kevin said. "You can't really prove she sent the emails. They didn't come from her email account."

"They didn't?" Matt asked, looking confused.

"How do you know that?" Eamon demanded, studying Kevin, looking for deception in his shifty gaze.

Kevin blinked. "Well, because ... dude, you showed me the email."

"I showed you the photo attachment," Eamon said. "I never showed you the actual emails. So, again, how do you know the emails didn't come from her account?"

"He probably figured because, you know, she's smart ..." Matt stammered, a pained expression on his flushed face. "She wouldn't send anything from her real email account."

"I'd like to hear Kevin's answer." Eamon persisted, regretting his decision to refrain from punching Kevin. "How do you know—"

"Dude, it's like Matt said," Kevin said. "She's a smart woman. She's not stupid enough to email you from her real account. She's gotta have plausible deniability in case you go to HR. That way, she can say, hey, I'm being set up. I didn't send these emails. This is a fake email account."

Eamon exhaled, worried, knowing Kevin was right. "So what the hell can I do?"

Shaking his head, Matt said, "Dude, what she's doing is harassment."

Kevin nodded in agreement. "It does suck, bro. Sorry for making light of it, okay? Kinda is a huge problem and I guess I don't know what you can do. Going to HR might be your only option, as risky as it is."

"Well, I'll tell you what I'm not going to do." Eamon took another long swig of his Felipe beer. "I'm not going to lose my job because of some horny bitch. She's not going to fuck with me and get away with it."

As he finished his beer, Eamon caught the worried look Matt shot at Kevin, but he didn't care what they thought about him. He was sure they secretly viewed him as a Handweg hoodlum and expected him to be aggressive and intimidating. Their opinions didn't matter. What mattered was his life and everything he'd worked so hard to obtain.

He'd fought damn hard to get out of Handweg Gardens, the island ghetto where he felt like a prisoner, longing to escape the oppressive expectations of a community doomed to poverty. Marginalized and disenfranchised, the residents of Handweg were content to accept their sorry state, depending on the government for handouts. Even without role models to encourage him, Eamon had decided he wouldn't end up as a Handweg statistic.

"She's not going to ruin my life," Eamon vowed.

"No, Dr. Bean probably won't ruin your life," said Kevin, pulling something from his pocket. "But, I know someone who can."

"Who?" asked Matt. "Sarah?"

"No, not her," said Kevin, tossing what he'd removed from his pocket at Eamon.

Eamon made the catch and stared at the small envelope. His name was scrawled in a looping script he recognized.

"I was asked to deliver that to you," said Kevin, a slight suspicion in his narrowed eyes.

Shoving the envelope into the back pocket of his jeans, Eamon said, "As I was saying, Dr. Bean is not going to fuck with me and get away with it."

As Kevin and Matt provided him with more of their unsolicited opinions about his predicament with Dr. Bean, Eamon thought about the envelope in his pocket.

Later, when he was alone, he would read the letter even though he knew the words would be disturbing and frightening ...

Chapter Ten

Noelle Bean slumped down in the chair at the desk in her office.

Famished and frustrated, she made a few clicks with her computer mouse to open a database software she needed to update. Work today had been insane. Crazy busy. She'd barely had time for lunch, let alone a quick break to catch her breath in between verifying prescriptions, administering flu shots, working the pharmacy consultation window and filling hundreds of prescriptions.

Right about now, all she wanted was a Felipe beer and a foot rub, compliments of Beanie who would most likely make his way up her legs and in between them. Giggling, feeling a bit naughty, she let her mind wander to their date night three days ago. Their blistering hot sex in the car had been just the beginning. At home, they'd engaged in more lovemaking after Sarah Linde had left and they'd made sure the boys were still sleeping.

Staring at her computer, Noelle sighed. She was anxious to get home, but she had a few more administrative duties to wrap up before she could leave. Her staff today—two pharmacy techs and a part-time pharmacist who came in when Eamon Taylor wasn't scheduled to work—had left an hour ago.

After inputting information into the database, Noelle opened a Word file to create a memo for—

A knock on the office door made her jump. Startled, Noelle looked over her shoulder.

Grady Palmer stood in the doorway.

"How the hell did you get in here?" Noelle stood, trying to remember if she'd set the alarm after the last pharmacy technician had left for the day. She thought she had. It was part of her normal routine, but she'd been so busy she might have forgotten to lock the door. Or, had the tech told her that she would lock it on her way out?

Didn't matter. Grady Palmer was here now, at her job. On her turf. She would have to defend her space. In Handweg Gardens, where the gang mentality still thrived, certain roads were the unofficial territory of certain gangs or criminal factions. You couldn't just take a leisurely stroll without explaining why you were walking down that block. Grady Palmer had to know he couldn't walk down her street.

Grady smiled at her, the same menacing smile he'd given her two months ago when she'd seen him for the first time in fifteen years.

Noelle had been at the bank to order more checks for her mother, who wasn't computer savvy and didn't trust online banking to pay bills, when she'd seen him. Leaning on the trunk of her car, a red mid-sized sedan she'd bought to run errands, he was smiling and sinister.

Staring at him in disbelief, Noelle had thought her heart might stop. Grady Palmer. She hadn't seen or heard from him in fifteen years. What the hell could he possibly want? And why now? She'd been back in St. Killian for five years. Aside from one or two old acquaintances, no one from her old neighborhood had tried to contact her since she'd returned.

Grady Palmer had been a foreboding presence that Thursday afternoon. Like a storm cloud encroaching on a lovely day, he was a menace she'd hoped never to encounter again.

But, there he'd been, demanding and intimidating, trying to get her involved in some wicked scheme on behalf of the violent island gang organization he belonged to—the PC-5.

In the sixties, when the Palmchat Islands had been in a civil rights struggle, yearning for its independence from the European country which had claimed and colonized it centuries ago, five freedom fighters had been on the front lines of the battle.

Originally, the five civil rights proponents created the PC-5 to organize and fund protest marches. They'd staged several uprisings where oppressed, and marginalized native St. Killians were armed with guns the PC-5 had brokered in deals with South American drug cartels.

The five freedom fighters had forayed into illegal and illicit activities to bankroll their mission of independence. Freedom meant access to good schools, adequate housing, jobs and a greater presence in the island's government affairs.

However, after independence was won, the descendants of the PC-5 decided to exploit the criminal connections made by their ancestors. Through threats and violence, they expanded their illegal enterprise which currently was centered around gambling, drugs, prostitution and protection rackets.

A Handweg Hoodlum from birth, Grady had started off as a lookout, watching for cops during PC-5 drug deals. He became a mule next, carrying drugs from stash houses to the streets, and then, through a series of violent acts of self-promotion, he became a faction leader and was put in charge of a crew comprised mostly of mules and lookouts under his direction.

Noelle suspected unrelenting ambition had gotten the best of him. Looking to move up in the PC-5, he probably hoped to rule the gang's St. Killian operations. Fifteen years ago, when she was entranced by his intimidating swagger and thought she might be falling in love with him, Grady used to share his dreams of rising to the top of the PC-5, running the entire organization.

A ridiculous pipe dream. Grady had to know he would never be more than a high-level faction leader. Top tier leadership positions—like the head of the St. Killian PC-5—were reserved exclusively for legacy members. Referring to themselves as thugs-in-law, they were blood descendants and relatives of the gang's original "founding five."

"So, Dr. Bean," Grady said, saying her title as though he thought it was a dubious distinction. "You gonna help me out? Surely by now, you've made your decision. I've given you more than enough time."

"I already told you," Noelle said, prepared to stand her ground. "I can't help you. What you want me to do is illegal."

"It's not illegal to fill a prescription," said Grady, leaning against the door jam, his tone casual, as though he weren't asking her to do something that would risk her livelihood.

"It's illegal when it's a prescription written by a fake doctor," Noelle said. "It's illegal when the customer doesn't really need the medicine."

The scam wasn't just illegal; it was crazy. Grady wanted her to fill bogus prescriptions for highly-addictive opioids, like OxyContin, Vicodin, and hydrocodone.

According to Grady, it would be a simple and easy system. He would have someone in his crew bring her several prescriptions. She would fill them, and the crew member would take the powerful pain medication back to Grady, who planned to sell them.

Advancing toward her, Grady stopped inches away, close enough to smell his nicotine-scented breath and the cheap cologne he'd never stopped wearing.

"Mrs. Bean, you need to think about what you're going to do," Grady said. "There's a wrong decision and a right decision you can make. The right decision can put a little cash in your pocket while you're helping out an old friend."

"I'm not your friend."

"You used to be," he said, stepping closer, forcing her to step back. "We used to have some good times together Nobody."

"I'm not Nobody," she said, glaring at him.

"Yeah, I guess you think you're somebody now," he said. "You went to college, and now you have a good job and a family. You need to think about your family. They need you to be somebody. But, if you make the wrong decision, you won't just be nobody, you'll be nothing. I'll make sure of that."

Trembling with rage, she held his gaze. In Handweg Gardens, if you looked away from an opponent, enemy or rival, you were considered weak. Grady had to know she wasn't afraid of him. He couldn't break her with scare tactics.

"I'll give you another week to make the right decision," Grady said.

"Don't make your husband and your little boys suffer for your stupid mistakes."

After another cruel smile, he turned and strode toward the door.

Anger rushing through her, Noelle grabbed a stapler from her desk and hurled it at the back of Grady's head. The staple gun hit its target, striking with a dull thud.

Grady spun around and was on her in an instant, hitting her across the face, a vicious back-handed slap, sending her across the small office.

Banging against a tall file cabinet, Noelle fought to get her bearings as terror replaced the anger. Why had she hit Grady? She knew how violent he could be; she remembered the times when he would—

Grady's hand clamped around her neck, pressing into her throat as he pinned her against the file cabinet. Eyes wild and furious, he glared at her. "That was a stupid thing to do, Dr. Bean," he said through gritted teeth, his voice a low growl. "You better be glad I need your help, or I would break your damn neck."

Struggling to breathe, her heart thundering, Noelle looked away from his enraged gaze. She no longer cared if he thought she was weak. She just wanted him to release her, to let her live to see Beanie and the boys again.

Attacking him had been a dumb move; a Handweg Ho reaction— one that could have gotten her killed.

With a grunt, Grady removed his hand and shoved her. "Crazy bitch," he muttered on his way out.

Rubbing her neck, Noelle coughed and then took deep breaths. Even though she shook uncontrollably, she felt paralyzed, not sure what she should do next. Putting one foot in front of the other, the very act of moving from the spot where she was rooted seemed daunting.

After a few more coughs, she cleared her throat. Grady's endeavor couldn't be accomplished. She would be caught and end up in jail, away from her family. And then she would be nothing, a nobody once again.

Grady's cruel threats against Beanie and the boys were horrifying, but no matter what, she could not let Grady hurt her family. She had to do whatever it took to protect them. Even if whatever it took meant breaking the law.

With a shuddering breath, feeling helpless and hopeless, Noelle sank to the floor and sobbed.

Chapter Eleven

Listless and lethargic, Noelle shuffled into the kitchen.

Last night, still trembling and terrified from Grady Palmer's attack, she'd feigned a headache to avoid Beanie and the boys. Beanie sensed her distress and told her he would take care of getting the boys fed and off to bed while she relaxed. His compassion and understanding touched her. She didn't deserve his sensitivity, but she took advantage of it and hurried into the shower.

As the hot pounding spray of water drowned out her sobs, Noelle berated herself, feeling like a fraud. Helen Farber had been right about her—she was a con woman, pretending to be something she wasn't, a successful professional unencumbered by a past she should have known would come back to haunt her.

Eventually, she recovered enough to towel off and slip into a pair of pajamas. Unable to bring herself to kiss the boys goodnight, she'd crawled into bed, drowning in hopelessness. Hours later, when Beanie slipped in next to her, she allowed him to wrap his arms around her. Unable to resist his comfort, Noelle had resolved to deal with her problems the next day.

Noelle exhaled, irritated by the bright sunshine streaming through the kitchen windows. She'd continued the headache ruse this morning. Even though Noelle wasn't scheduled to work today, Beanie agreed to leave early to drop the kids off at her mother's house before he went to work.

Sniffing, Noelle wiped away tears before they had a chance to fall. She hated lying to her husband, but what choice did she have? She couldn't tell Beanie about Grady Palmer's threats. He would demand to know why Grady had come to her with his illegal proposal and she couldn't tell him the truth. Couldn't tell him about her past with Grady. She couldn't tell him about her past—period.

If Beanie knew the truth about her, he might not trust her anymore. He might not think she was good enough to be the mother of his children. The familiar dread passed through her, almost bringing her to her knees. What if Beanie left her? What if he took the kids from her? She wouldn't survive. She would die without her children.

Taking a deep breath, Noelle forced herself to calm down. She couldn't drive herself crazy jumping to wild conclusions. Beanie wasn't going to leave her, and she wasn't going to lose her children because she was going to deal with Grady Palmer. Someway. Somehow.

After starting the coffee maker, she leaned against the counter. She was thankful for the day off, and yet she couldn't bear the thought of being alone with her helpless lament, surging anger, and confusion. Usually, on her days off from the pharmacy, Noelle would be energized and enterprising, running errands, preparing lesson plans and lecture notes. She had a feeling today would be wasted ruminating on Grady Palmer's unreasonable demands.

Finished with her first cup of coffee, Noelle decided to tackle the dishes Beanie had left in the sink. Staring at the dirty ceramic plates, she guessed the boys had been treated to frozen pizza. Noelle couldn't help but smile. Whenever Beanie made dinner for the kids, he conveniently forgot to add vegetables to the meal.

She opened the dishwasher and then grabbed the first plate from the pile.

Beneath the plate, a large butcher's knife lay on top of a plastic cutting board.

Red smears stained the blade.

Hands shaking, Noelle picked up the knife. Was it a sign? Did she really have to kill Grady Palmer? Was that the answer? She'd thought about ending his life. Maybe killing the bastard was the only way to get him out of hers. But, could she really do it? Could she put a knife in his chest? Did she have a choice?

Heart slamming, Noelle turned away from the sink.

When she was younger, before she left St. Killian for a better life, she'd done terrible things. She'd made bad decisions and had gotten caught up in dangerous situations, but ... she'd never killed anyone. Was she even capable of murder?

If it meant saving her family then ... she would have to.

Turning back to the sink, Noelle stared at the stainless steel blade. Pomegranate seeds. Beanie must have made the boys pomegranate smoothies, their favorite. Noelle took a deep breath. She put the knife and the remaining dishes in the dishwasher, then closed the door and set it to run.

She was heading to the coffee maker for a second cup when the doorbell rang. Who the hell? Pinching the bridge of her nose, she contemplated ignoring the door but then decided the visitor might be a welcome distraction.

As she opened the door, for a split second, panic washed over her. What if Grady Palmer was at her door?

"Dr. Noelle Bean?" asked a young, skinny, tawny-skinned St. Killian guy wearing khaki Bermuda shorts and a polo shirt with the logo: PCI Deliveries.

"Yes?" Curious and confused, Noelle tightened the belt on her robe. "I'm Dr. Bean."

"Delivery for you," said the guy, handing her a #10 envelope.

After signing for it, Noelle barely mumbled her thanks and closed the door. The chill of dread increasing within her, Noelle stood in the foyer, staring at the return address: Alexio and Gaston, Attorneys at Law. Frowning, her heart rate climbing, Noelle opened the letter.

After reading it once, she had to read it again, and then a third time. Still, she didn't understand what the hell was going on. Barely able to breathe, Noelle read the letter a fourth time. Was this some kind of joke? Heat spiraled up her neck, scorching and stifling.

Furious, she stared at the letter, tempted to shred it to pieces. She didn't know why the hell this letter had been sent to her, but she was for damn sure going to find out.

Chapter Twelve

"Where the hell is Eamon?" Noelle demanded, stalking toward the front counter. The startled pharmacy tech, who was counting the till at the cash register, stammered something that sounded like *storage room*.

To the far right of the counter, at the door marked EMPLOYEES ONLY, Noelle swiped her access badge. Grabbing the knob, she yanked the door open and headed behind the counter, her anger increasing with each step.

Once the shock and confusion of the letter had worn off, seething rage had taken over Noelle as words and phrases from the attorney circled in her mind like buzzards over carrion.

My name is Attorney George Gaston ... Our firm represents Mr. Eamon Taylor. Recently, Mr. Taylor has retained our firm ... informed our firm that you have been transmitting harassing messages of a sexual, lewd and salacious manner via electronic mail ... he decided to forgo causing any embarrassment to the company, yourself or your family ... please contact our firm ... We thank you in advance ... and look forward to hearing from you immediately to remedy this grievance.

Behind several shelving units, at the rear of the dispensary, Noelle found Eamon, another pharmacy technician, and a part-time pharmacist at the back counter laughing as they filled prescriptions from the overnight queue.

As she stomped toward the trio, the pharmacy tech glanced over her shoulder, saw Noelle and began to smile, but wasn't quite able to complete the action.

"Dr. Bean?" The pharmacy tech stared at her, wide eyes confused. "What are you doing here? I thought—"

"Eamon," Noelle called out to him, pointing the letter at him. "What the hell is this?"

Eamon's shoulders slumped and then squared before he faced her. His face impassive, he stared at her.

"What the hell do you mean by having these asshole lawyers send me this bullshit letter?" Noelle stalked closer to him, ignoring the furtive, bewildered stares of the tech and the part-time pharmacist who both shrank back, seemingly unsure of what they should do.

Glancing back and forth at their frightened co-workers, Eamon said, "I don't think we should discuss this right now."

"I don't give a damn what you think," Noelle said, jabbing the letter toward him. "You are going to tell me what the fuck you are trying to pull with these ridiculous lies!"

Flinching, Eamon stepped back. "I'm not lying. You know what you did. I have proof."

"You have proof of something I didn't do?" Noelle asked. "Because you know that I didn't send you any—"

"Dr. Bean, please ..." Eamon cut her off. "I don't think we need to discuss this in front of—"

"So, what the hell is your plan?" Noelle demanded. "You're going to sue me?"

"Did you read the letter?" Eamon asked. "I don't want to sue you. I want to work this out. I want—"

"You want to ruin my life!" Noelle said. "You want to destroy my career and everything I've worked for! Why, Eamon? You want my job? Is that it?"

"I don't want your job, Dr. Bean," Eamon insisted. "I am very happy with my job—"

"Which you only have because of me!" Noelle reminded him. "I chose you out of all the applicants. I chose you over applicants who were probably more qualified than you! Nevertheless, I saw something very enterprising and industrious in you, but I was obviously completely wrong about you!"

"Dr. Bean, I appreciate that you believed in me," Eamon said. "But, if you think that I owe you because you gave me a job—"

"All I ever asked or wanted was for you to be appreciative of this job ..." she said. "And to work hard and—"

"You wanted way more than that, Dr. Bean ... you wanted more than I can give you," Eamon said. "You wanted way too much, and I can't let you get away with what you're doing. It's wrong."

"You know what, Eamon," Noelle said. "I don't know what kind of scam you're trying to pull, but it's not going to work! You are not going to ruin my life!"

"I am not trying to ruin your life or your career, Dr. Bean," Eamon said. "I don't want to sue you and drag your name through the mud which would embarrass your family."

"Don't pretend like you give a shit about my family or me," Noelle said.

"You know what, Dr. Bean?" Scowling, Eamon took a step toward her. "I'm trying to be civil about this, but I could have been ruthless and cutthroat. I could have been a straight-up Handweg Hoodlum, but I decided not to because I believe we can resolve this situation calmly and rationally."

"Calmly and rationally?" Noelle shook her head. "How the hell can I be calm and rational when you are a lying piece of shit accusing me of something I would never do?"

"Obviously, we're not going to be able to have a civil conversation about this right now," said Eamon. "I think the best thing would be for you to contact my lawyers and—"

"Here's what would be the best thing for you to do, Eamon," Noelle said. "Watch your damn back. You messed with the wrong person! Don't ever try to dig a grave for me because you will be the one who gets buried in it!"

Chapter Thirteen

"Son of a bitch!" Beanie ranted, pacing across the kitchen. "Who the hell does he think he is? He can't get away with this bullshit! He's a damn liar!"

At the center island, Noelle focused on chopping florets from the head of broccoli she planned to steam as a healthy compliment to the mashed potatoes and goat fritters.

Noelle agreed. The son of a bitch couldn't get away with his bull-shit lies. She was just as enraged as Beanie was, but not about the same person. Beanie was kvetching about his editor, Leo Bronson, who had ripped the entire reporting staff a new one today. As she chopped, lulled by the rhythm of the knife against the cutting board, Noelle tried to pay attention to Beanie, but her mind kept wondering.

She couldn't stop thinking about the letter from Alexio and Gaston, Attorneys-at-Law. Shoved into the back of her jeans, the offensive missive felt as though it was burning a hole in the denim.

"Babe, you okay?"

Glancing up, she said, "Yeah ... I'm fine."

"You seem distracted," Beanie said, standing on the opposite side of the island

Noelle shook her head, still chopping florets. "Just upset about your bad day."

"Well, don't take it out on the broccoli."

"Hmmm."

"You're mincing those florets," said Beanie, smiling.

"Oh ..." Noelle fought tears as she stared at the florets, which now resembled chopped parsley. Struggling to fight hopeless frustration, she said, "Well, I was thinking of mixing the broccoli into the mashed potatoes."

Beanie's gaze was skeptical, but he nodded. "That should be good."

"Let's hope," said Noelle, glancing at the ruined broccoli, feeling like a failure.

"Anyway, enough with my complaining," Beanie said. "How was your day?"

Noelle froze for a moment. She didn't know how to answer him. She couldn't tell Beanie about the letter from Attorney Gaston or her Handweg Ho reaction to it, which she deeply regretted, and was embarrassed about.

What would Beanie think if she told him? Noelle was certain he would share her outrage. Beyond his indignation and confusion would be one dominating question: Why would Eamon accuse her of sexually harassing him? What could Noelle say? She had no idea why Eamon was accusing her of something so horrible. Would Beanie believe her? Or would he secretly wonder if there was any truth to Eamon's ludicrous claims against her? Noelle couldn't bear the idea of Beanie having doubts about her. She didn't want him worrying, either, or getting upset or vowing to kill Eamon.

The situation was depressing and debilitating, but she would handle it. Somehow. She would meet with Eamon's attorneys. She would prove, someway, that she couldn't have harassed Eamon. She would convince his lawyers that Eamon's accusation was a vicious lie designed to ruin her reputation.

Noelle decided to avoid Beanie's question so she wouldn't have to lie. "Hey, can you go check on the boys? I'll have dinner ready in twenty minutes, or so."

Beanie gave her a quick kiss before he left the kitchen.

Noelle drifted to the sink and gazed out the window at the roses she'd planted last week. Sighing, she wiped away the tears as they rolled down her cheeks. Why was this happening to her? Why was her life going to hell? What had she done wrong to make so many terrible things happen to her at once? She couldn't help but think—

Your whole world is going to fall apart right before your eyes, and there won't be anything you can do to stop it.

Turning from the kitchen window, Noelle rubbed her arms as Helen Farber's portentous words sent a shudder of dread through her.

Chapter Fourteen

"The bitch is definitely out to get me," Eamon said as he paced around the thread-bare second-hand couch his aunt had given him. "She pretty much threatened to kill me!"

"Bro, chill," said Kevin, stretching out across the lumpy cushions as he opened his second Felipe beer. "Dr. Bean didn't threaten to kill you."

"She said she would bury me in a fucking grave," said Eamon.

"But only if you tried to dig a grave for her," said Kevin, reminding Eamon of Dr. Bean's exact quote. "It was more of a counter to your direct threat against her."

"Actually, it was a conditional threat predicated upon a specific action from Eamon—digging the grave to bury Dr. Bean." Matt pointed out. "She's only gonna bury you if you try to bury her first."

Kevin took another swig of beer and said, "Which you did."

"How the hell did I try to bury Dr. Bean?" Eamon asked. "She sexually harassed me! I wasn't trying to bury her, even though I could have. I didn't go to HR, which I should have done, and I didn't sue her, which, again, I should have done. Instead, I offered to work things out fairly and discreetly."

Kevin snorted. "You want her to pay you to keep quiet and use her influence to get you transferred to another location. Not sure if she would think that was fair."

"That seems like a reasonable resolution to me," said Matt, slouching in the recliner, staring at his smartphone. "Dr. Bean might agree to that especially since it means she won't lose her job or have her reputation trashed."

Shrugging, Kevin said, "Bro, don't get pissed but I can see why Dr. Bean thinks you're scamming her."

Eamon glared at Kevin, tempted to snatch the beer bottle from his hand, smash it against the coffee table and slash his smug face.

"Look at the situation from Dr. Bean's point of view," suggested Kevin. "You come at her with accusations of sexual harassment, for which you claim you have proof, but—"

"I do have proof," Eamon insisted.

Kevin said, "But you didn't show her the proof."

"Because my lawyers advised me not to," Eamon said. "They told me if I mentioned the emails then she would immediately mount a defense claiming the emails were fake."

"Because they are fake," Kevin said.

"The photo was doctored, yeah," Eamon conceded. "But the emails are real. She sent them. My lawyers say we can trace the emails using the IP address. We can prove the emails were sent from her computer even if the email address isn't hers."

"Unless she didn't send the emails from her computer," said Matt.

"Exactly," said Kevin. "We've already established that Dr. Bean is a smart woman. She probably sent those emails from a computer in some Internet café from a burner phone that can't be traced."

"My lawyers are confident the emails will be traced back to Dr. Bean." Eamon rubbed his neck, trying not to worry, but he felt considerably less confident in the ability of his attorneys to prove his claims. He hadn't given up hope, but he had to consider the possibility that Dr. Bean might get away with harassing him.

"As I was saying," said Kevin. "It probably seems like a scam to Dr. Bean because she hasn't seen the proof."

"She already knows what my proof is because she sent the damn emails," Eamon said. "She doesn't really think I'm scamming her.

That's going to be her defense. She's going to lie and say she didn't send the emails. She's going to accuse me of sending them because I'm running some scheme to steal her job, which is bullshit."

"Bro, look, it's just the three of us here," Kevin said, voice lowered. "You can tell the truth. Me and Matt won't rat you out."

"What are you talking about?" Matt asked.

"That's what I want to know," Eamon said.

"Did Dr. Bean really send you those emails?" Kevin asked. "Or did you fake them so you could—"

"Get the fuck out of here!" Eamon went to the door and opened it. "Now!"

Kevin exhaled and stood. "Bro, listen, I'm not judging you. I get why you would do it. You have student loans and—"

Eamon stalked toward Kevin, anxious to beat the shit out of him.

"We're leaving." Matt jumped up, blocking Eamon's approach as he grabbed Kevin's arm. "Come on, dude, let's go."

Kevin finished his beer then tossed the empty bottle on the couch. "For the record," Kevin said. "I don't believe Dr. Bean tried to harass you. She tried to help your sorry ass, and you repay her kindness and generosity by—"

Eamon lunged at Kevin, but Matt pushed Kevin out of the way, sending him stumbling, laughing as he tried to avoid tripping over the coffee table.

"He's not worth it," said Matt, an apology in his gaze.

"Get his ass out of here," Eamon said as he took a deep breath and a few steps back.

Standing outside the doorway after he'd pushed Kevin out of the apartment, Matt shook his head. "Sorry, man. He's a douche sometimes."

Eamon nodded, trying to control his anger and ignore the urge to go after Kevin.

"I'm sure your lawyers will prove that you're telling the truth," said Matt. "Don't worry."

Alone in his apartment, Eamon picked up the empty beer bottle and hurled it at the door.

Chapter Fifteen

As her fingers flew over the keyboard, Noelle cringed, recalling the confrontation with Eamon.

Standing at the counter where prescriptions were filled, in the same area where she'd screamed at Eamon two days ago, her mortification knew no bounds. The impromptu vacation days hadn't been as relaxing as she'd hoped, but at least she didn't have to face her co-workers. She suspected, however, that forty-eight hours wasn't enough time to forget the hostile scene.

How could she have been so unprofessional? She'd never behaved that way before in her entire career. As a supervisor, Noelle was well aware of the established company protocols when there was any conflict between co-workers.

She should have spoken to Eamon in private instead of screaming expletives at him in front of other employees. Noelle cringed again, thinking about the pharmacy tech and the part-time pharmacist. She'd put them in an uncomfortable position. They hadn't deserved to witness her irrational ire. What did they think of her now? Maybe that they didn't really know her. She wasn't the woman they'd believed her to be.

She was—

A con artist ...

Helen Farber, in her head again. Maybe the twisted bitch was right. Maybe Dr. Noelle Bean was just pretending to be the dutiful wife, adoring mother and successful career woman. Maybe Noelle was really Nobody—the girl from the wrong side of the island. A girl with a rough upbringing whose natural instincts demanded she go on the attack and defend herself if she was confronted. She thought she'd left the Handweg attitude behind but obviously not considering how quickly those old street life tendencies had come roaring back.

Noelle took a deep breath. She'd arrived at work an hour before her staff usually showed up so she could catch up on prescriptions that had been called in after hours, but she couldn't focus. Usually, she could get lost in the methodical monotony of her job, but she couldn't stop thinking about that damn letter from Eamon's lawyers.

The letter had almost stolen her attention from Ethan and Evan. She'd spent her vacation days trying to focus on them and trying not to dwell on the hell she was experiencing because of Eamon Taylor. In the back of her mind, as she played with her precious little men, Noelle knew she would have to call Attorney Gaston to set up a meeting soon, or Eamon might—

"Noelle ..."

Startled, Noelle turned. Sigmund Benz, the manager responsible for the fifteen Palmchat Pharmacy locations across the Palmchat chain, walked toward her, his stride stiff and hesitant.

"I didn't expect you to be here this early. I thought I would have to wait for you to show up but no matter. Are you alone?" Sigmund asked, his expression pinched with concern. "When do you expect your staff?"

"Not for an hour, or so," Noelle said, hearing the tremor in her voice as her heart hammered. "I'm alone. I didn't know you were going to stop by ..."

"I hadn't planned to, but there has been a disturbing development."

Noelle swallowed, praying her voice wouldn't fail. "A disturbing development."

"We must speak about this situation immediately," Sigmund said, "as it involves you ... and Eamon Taylor."

Chapter Sixteen

The day ended as it began, with Noelle standing at the workstation where she filled prescriptions, her fingers flying over the keyboard.

The pharmacy had closed two hours ago, and her staff was long gone, but Noelle hadn't been in a hurry to leave. There was a lot to do and she'd always taken pride in the location's ability to fill scripts promptly. Over the years, the St. Killian store had received several awards and accolades for outstanding customer service thanks in part to Noelle's tireless devotion and willingness to put in extra hours. When she'd first started her career, Noelle would often stay late to impress her superiors and showcase her strong work ethics.

Today, however, she wasn't trying to be super-pharmacist.

She hesitated to go home because as soon as she walked through the door, Beanie and the boys would steal her attention which she was usually eager to give them. But, she needed to think. Work had been hectic. There hadn't been a moment for even a minute of reflection on the situation with Eamon and his false accusations.

The impromptu visit from Sigmund Benz still rattled her when she replayed it in her mind. Noelle had barely been able to concentrate on what Benz was saying. His dour expression and dire tone sent her pulse racing so fast; she thought she might faint. Somehow, she'd managed to walk with Benz to her office where, behind closed doors, he confirmed her fears.

With grave solemnity, he'd informed her of a notification he'd received from the Human Resources department.

"Eamon Taylor resigned his position this morning."

"Eamon resigned?" Noelle's mouth went dry. "Why?"

"Mr. Taylor claims he was ..." Benz had hesitated before saying, "sexually harassed ... by you."

Noelle had been glad she was sitting down.

"Noelle, what is going on?" Benz asked. "Why would Mr. Taylor say such a thing about you? Surely, his claims aren't true ... are they?"

"Benz, you have to believe me," Noelle said. "There is no truth to these claims. They are completely unfounded and unprovoked."

Noelle wasn't sure Benz believed her. The regional manager seemed to be struggling to mask his skepticism, but she didn't know for sure. She and Benz had always been friendly, cordial, and admiring of each other's accomplishments. He'd always lauded her success and held her in high esteem, but was he disappointed?

She'd searched his face, looking for subtle signs of disgust but his expression was passive, betraying nothing.

Sigmund Benz told Noelle he was scheduled to have a meeting with HR and the company lawyers about the matter and would get back to her.

After Benz left, Noelle wasn't sure what to think.

Eamon's resignation had floored her. She couldn't help thinking he'd quit the job because he was going to file a lawsuit against her—and probably the company, too. Noelle wanted to kick herself for not contacting Attorney George Gaston and resolving the issue. She could have paid Eamon off and recommended him to a pharmacy in St. Mateo. Or St. Felipe. Or Cera. Eamon could be out of her life right now. She wouldn't have to worry about losing her job.

Noelle wished she knew if Benz had believed her.

She'd always known Sigmund Benz to be unemotional and stoic, but fair and impartial, only interested in facts supported by irrefutable evidence.

Benz wouldn't jump to conclusions, but he would conduct a thorough investigation in his effort to get the truth. More than anyone, Noelle knew the truth wasn't always as it appeared. The truth could mislead and deceive. It could manipulate and misinform. The truth couldn't always be relied on to provide answers.

Eamon claimed he had proof of her harassment and Noelle didn't doubt it. Eamon probably did have evidence to back up his claim, but his proof wasn't real. It might, however, be authentic enough to appear real.

Noelle pinched the bridge of her nose and tried not to fidget. Eamon's so-called proof worried her. What if Benz and the HR director believed the fake evidence?

Looping the cross-body purse over her head, Noelle grabbed her briefcase. She set the pharmacy's alarm and exited the door that opened to the back alley, a wide two-lane strip of dirt road behind the retail center where the pharmacy shared space with a dry cleaner's, and ice cream shop, and a dentist who sent all of his patients to the pharmacy for pain medication.

She closed the heavy door, which locked automatically from the inside. Turning, she shielded her eyes from the coppery late afternoon sun and headed to her car, backed against the chain-link fence which separated the alley from the empty lot, overgrown with trees and bushes, behind it.

She couldn't drive herself crazy worrying about the meeting between Benz and the HR director, Noelle decided. She would go insane playing the "what if" game. She had to try her best not to jump to conclusions and imagine the worst.

Beanie and the boys would help keep her mind off the worst. She just had to focus on what was most important in her life, count her many blessings and—

A hand pressed against her mouth. What the hell was happening? Her heart shot into her throat and would have exited her mouth if the hand wasn't preventing her from screaming. Struggling against the arm clamped around her chest, Noelle couldn't help but think of Grady Palmer. Was he behind this attack? Was this a brutal message? Had he sent one of his PC-5 thugs to scare her into compliance?

"Give me the keys, bitch!" The keys? Confusion spread through her, clouding the fear. What was going on? Was she being carjacked? Violently, Noelle pitched forward, slipping on the gravel as she realized the assailant had pushed her. Turning, she cried out for help as she stumbled, trying to get her bearings. Dressed in jeans and a dark T-shirt, and wearing what looked like a white hockey mask, the attacker lunged at her. Noelle swung her briefcase, whacking him against the arm. Cursing her, he grabbed the briefcase, tossed it aside, and back-handed her across the face.

Startled by the stinging blow, Noelle stumbled to her left, lost her footing and crashed down on one knee. Pain spiraled up her leg as she struggled to get to her feet, praying he wouldn't kick her, or—

"Give me the keys!"

Noelle glanced up at him and froze.

The attacker pointed a gun at her. "I want the keys now!"

Through gasping pants, she whispered, "The keys are in my purse."

"Get them out and give them to me," he said, "or I will put a bullet in your head."

With trembling fingers, Noelle grabbed the zipper of the cross-body purse she'd looped around her shoulder, yanked it open and pulled out the keys.

"Put them on the ground and then get on your stomach and keep your fucking head down!"

Crying, she complied, her body shaking as she flattened out on the dirt road. Terrified he would shoot her in the back of the head even though she'd obeyed him, Noelle forced herself to stay as still as she could.

The car engine roared to life. Tires squealed, churning up a spray of dust and hot exhaust. Pelted with gravel, Noelle coughed and scrambled to her knees. Sobbing, Noelle watched the glowing taillights blur as the car sped through the back alley. The Honda fishtailed as the carjacker turned the corner on two wheels, and disappeared down the side street.

Shaking, Noelle sat in the dirt, trying to breathe, unsure of what to do. She tried to scream for help, but her voice was a plaintive, hoarse whisper. She looked around. The alley was empty. There was no one to help her. No one who had witnessed the attack. She took another deep breath. Beanie. She needed Beanie. He would know what to do. Pushing a hand down into her purse, Noelle pulled out her phone.

For a few moments, she stared at the phone, trying to remember Beanie's phone number. Close to hysteria, she searched the contacts, found her husband's number and dialed it. As the phone rang, she whispered prayers, thanking God that she hadn't been shot and left to bleed to death in the street.

Beanie answered the phone. "Hey, babe, where are—"

"Oh, thank God, Beanie ..." Noelle burst into tears. "Beanie, please come! Somebody robbed me! They stole my car! Please come now!"

Chapter Seventeen

Lounging in her favorite pajamas, Noelle sat at the kitchen table, sipping coffee, as she perused the *Palmchat Gazette*.

Beanie had a story on the front page, and she was immensely proud. Beanie said it would have been a bigger deal if the article had been "above the fold," but Noelle reminded him there was no "fold" on the Internet, which was where a growing majority of St. Killian residents read the paper.

Noelle skimmed a few more stories and then contemplated whether or not she wanted a third cup of coffee.

Usually, the opportunity to finish half a cup was a luxury, considering how busy she was at the pharmacy but she wasn't going to work today. She hadn't gone yesterday, or the day before that, either. Today would be her third day off since she'd been attacked in the alley behind the pharmacy and had her car stolen.

She shuddered, remembering the horror of that day. She still had nightmares about the gun and the hockey mask the thief had worn. She still wondered if the carjacking had been random or if Grady Palmer had ordered the attack to force her hand.

Three days should have been enough time to get herself together and get back to doing what she did best, but Noelle was still shaken up, nervous and jumpy. Truthfully, she wasn't eager to go back to the pharmacy just yet. She couldn't walk into the store without thinking about all of the horrible experiences she'd had there recently.

The visit from Grady Palmer had left her shattered and terrified. The confrontation with Eamon, when she'd been so unprofessional and vulgar, made her feel guilty and ashamed. Benz's visit had given her much to ponder and worry about. Was her career over? Would she be sued? Or fired? She hadn't heard from Benz or the HR director about the situation with Eamon so as far as she knew, the internal investigation was still ongoing.

The carjacking had nearly been her undoing, and if not for Beanie she wouldn't have survived these past days.

Since her attack, Beanie had been working from home and had scarcely left her side. As soon as she'd seen him running down the alley toward her, Noelle had known she could survive anything—a threat from her past, a false accusation, a gun in her face—as long as Beanie was by her side.Sunlight streaming into the kitchen promised another gorgeous morning in St. Killian. Noelle thought it might be a good day to finish planting her roses. A week or so ago, she'd been in the middle of the pet project when she realized she had to pick up the boys from her mother's house.

She'd planned to continue with the rose bush planting that weekend, but Saturday morning, she'd discovered someone had broken into the shed and stolen several garden tools—including her discounted shovel with the bent blade.

Noelle stood and walked to the coffee maker. Beanie was in the home office researching another story, and the boys were having a mid-morning nap. Maybe in an hour or so, the four of them could head down to the local hardware store and buy replacements for the tools that had been stolen.

Probably would be good to get out, Noelle reasoned as she crossed to the refrigerator to get the liquid creamer. Not only had she not been to work in three days, but she hadn't left the house during that time, so maybe—

The doorbell rang.

Noelle froze, her hand locked around the handle on the refrigerator door. Who could that be? What did they want? Her mind jumped to the worse conclusions. Was it Grady Palmer? Or some delivery guy with a legal summons telling her that she was being sued for sexual harassment? Or someone from the pharmacy with her termination papers? Or—

The doorbell rang a second time, and then a third. Panicked, Noelle removed her hand from the door handle. Maybe it was someone trying to sell something, or maybe—

"Babe, I'll get it!" She heard Beanie call out.

Noelle walked to the sink and stared out into the backyard. The roses she'd planted had started to bloom. As the red petals fluttered in the breeze, Noelle struggled to fight the foreboding feelings. She couldn't help thinking that the person at the door was there to ruin her life. As soon as Beanie opened the door, the fury of hell would come rushing in and—

"Babe, that was Officer Fields," Beanie said as he rushed into the kitchen, an air of tense excitement swirling around him as he walked toward her.

Noelle was confused. "Officer Fields?"

"The first responder who showed up after you were carjacked," Beanie reminded her, gently pulling her into his arms, staring at her. "The police think they found your car. They need us to come down to the station to identify it."

Chapter Eighteen

Roland Bean squeezed Noelle's hand as they sat on the loveseat in the conference room where a desk sergeant had instructed them to wait for Philippi Janvier, the detective assigned to Noelle's case.

The room was nice enough, Beanie supposed, with a picture window facing the Caribbean, casual, comfortable seating, and calming pale blue walls. A room designed to distract and deceive, Beanie figured, as it was probably where family members were given bad news about loved ones who were victims of horrific crimes.

As though a pretty room would lessen the trauma of finding out that someone you cared about had been brutally murdered, Beanie scoffed to himself. His thoughts pivoted, thinking about the purpose of the room, and he wondered if he and Noelle were about to be deceived, or—

"Mrs. Bean, how have you been since we last saw each other?" Detective Philippi Janvier said as he entered the small conference room. "Doing as well as can be expected, I assume, considering what happened to you, no?"

Beanie glanced at the detective, who was above-average height with a lean build, like a swimmer or a marathoner. Dressed in a wrinkled linen suit and clutching a blue file folder, Janvier exuded lack of confidence and ineptitude, but Beanie's colleague Caleb Olivier claimed the strange, salty Frenchman was a competent detective with a sharp, deductive mind.

Noelle nodded and started to speak, but Beanie cut her off, staring at Janvier as he said, "Doctor."

Sitting in the chair adjacent to the loveseat, Janvier looked confused. "I'm sorry?"

"She's Dr. Bean," said Beanie, though he was sure the detective knew that. The disrespect bothered Beanie as he suspected the detective had done it on purpose. Stripping Noelle of her accomplishments took away her authority. It was a control issue, Beanie knew, often used by law enforcement but it still pissed him off.

He wished Noelle's case had been assigned to Detective Baxter François, whom Beanie was familiar and friendly with, but they had to deal with this Janvier guy. Beanie didn't know much about him, but he didn't like the guy. Janvier was overly suspicious, for some reason. One of those cops who doubted the victim.

Three days ago, when he'd taken Noelle's statement after the carjacking Beanie hadn't liked his tone, which was distrustful, or his probing questions, which suggested a slight skepticism of Noelle's claims. Reflecting on the incident later, Beanie thought maybe he had taken offense when there had been none, allowing fear and frustration to distort his judgment.

As a journalist, he understood the need for doubt. There was always more to every story. Nevertheless, he didn't appreciate the suspicion Janvier had directed toward his wife, the victim, who deserved compassion and understanding.

"Officer Fields said you found Noelle's car," said Beanie, anxious to identify the vehicle so they could start the process to get the car returned.

"Yes, we are quite certain that we have found Dr. Bean's car," said Janvier, consulting the blue file which he held open so only he could see the contents. "A red 2011 Honda Civic. We have checked the plates, and VINs and the car we found is registered to Noelle Chartres Bean."

"What do I need to do to get my car back?" Noelle asked.

"What kind of condition is it in?" Beanie asked. "Did they strip it?"

"Actually, the car is in good working condition," said Janvier, still perusing his file. "We do not believe it was stolen so that parts could be removed from it and sold."

"Why do you think it was stolen?" Noelle asked.

"Was it used to commit a crime?" Beanie asked, his curiosity about Janvier's file growing into a mild apprehension. What the hell was the man looking at? Beanie had a feeling Janvier's interest in the file was an act. The detective appeared engrossed, but Beanie suspected Janvier was hesitating.

It reminded him of a reporter's trick, where you feigned distraction to give yourself time to think of your next question. Was that Janvier's game? Was there some question the detective wanted to ask, but he wasn't sure how because ... because of what? Beanie didn't know. He felt a fluttering of panic and kept his eyes on the detective, even though he could tell Noelle was glancing at him.

Interrogation, the business of questions and how to answer them, was Beanie's bread and butter. He wasn't a cop, but he was aware of certain examination techniques. He should have been able to determine what Janvier was trying to pull, but he was at a loss, and it worried him.

"Dr. Bean," started Janvier as he laid the blue file on the small end table between the loveseat and the chair. "May I ask, do you know a man named Eamon Taylor?"

"Eamon Taylor?" Noelle echoed, her voice hollow.

Beanie glanced at her, picking up on the surprise in her tone. There was a note of another emotion, as well, something he couldn't identify, something that increased his apprehension.

"Yes, Eamon Taylor," repeated Janvier. "Do you know him?"

Beanie looked at Noelle, and his heart jerked. Her wide-eyed expression, a mix of fear and dread, turned his slight apprehension into full-blown panic. What the hell was going on with Noelle? Why did she look so afraid? Why wasn't she saying anything?

Clearing his throat, desperate to cover for his wife, Beanie said, "Eamon Taylor is the intern who got the pharmacist assistant job, right?"

"Do you mind if Dr. Bean answers the question?" asked Janvier, his smile placating, full of pretense. He was playing the good cop, but Beanie wasn't fooled. He had a feeling Janvier was about to pull the rug from beneath them, but why?

"What does Eamon Taylor have to do with my car being stolen?" Noelle asked.

"Did Taylor steal Noelle's car?" Beanie demanded, leaning forward, staring at Janvier. "Did that bastard attack my wife?"

"Dr. Bean, I'd like to speak to you alone, if you don't mind?" Janvier posed the question directly to Noelle, ignoring Beanie.

"I do mind," Beanie said. "You're not talking to my wife without me being there."

"Mr. Bean—"

"It's okay, Beanie," said Noelle, squeezing his hand, a solemn resignation in her gaze as she tried to smile at him. "I'll be fine. Why don't you call my mom and see how the boys are doing?"

Beanie staged a valiant protest, but in the end, Noelle was adamant that she would be okay talking to the detective alone. Before she left, Beanie cautioned her not to answer any questions that made her uncomfortable or seemed inappropriate.

After a quick hug and kiss, Noelle left with Detective Janvier, giving Beanie a brave smile.

Twenty minutes later, Beanie was pacing the room, nervous and scared. What the hell was going on? Why did Janvier want to talk to Noelle alone? What the hell did Eamon Taylor have to do with the carjacking? Had he stolen Noelle's car? If so, why? Beanie had met the kid and Taylor seemed smart and enterprising. He'd grown up in Handweg Gardens, as Noelle had, and just like Noelle, he had escaped those tough streets. Maybe the guy was a Handweg Hood, after all. Maybe Eamon Taylor had everyone fooled.

An hour later, when Noelle hadn't returned, Beanie berated himself for allowing Janvier to question Noelle alone. He imagined his wife in some cold, sterile interrogation room, flinching and terrified as Janvier barked questions at her. Beanie couldn't understand what was happening. Officer Fields had told them to come to the station to identify Noelle's car. Fields hadn't mentioned anything about Eamon Taylor. What the hell was going on?

Beanie took a deep breath. Why the hell was he just standing there allowing questions to haunt him? He needed answers, and somebody was going to give them to him or—

The door opened, and Officer Fields rushed in. "Beanie—"

"Where's my wife?" Beanie demanded, his heart thundering. "What the hell—"

"Beanie, calm down," said Fields, concern in his gaze. "Listen to me, okay? I got bad news, man."

"Bad news?" Beanie felt his legs turn to mush. "What are you talking about? Where is Noelle?"

Fields exhaled. "She's been ... arrested."

"Arrested?" Beanie was confused. "I don't understand. Arrested for what? Having her car stolen?"

As though the words pained him, Fields said, "Noelle has been charged with first-degree murder in the death of Eamon Taylor."

Chapter Nineteen

"Beanie, oh my God, are you okay?" Sophie Carter, a junior reporter at the *Palmchat Gazette*, rushed toward Beanie as he walked into the newsroom for the first time in what felt like forever even though it had only been two days.

Two days of pure hell.

The two worst days of his life.

Following Sophie were Stevie Bishop and Caleb Olivier, friends and colleagues he respected. Woeful expressions betrayed their concern and worry.

"How's Noelle?" Stevie asked.

Beanie sighed, staring at his trio of co-workers, a strange emotion washing over him as he went to his desk. He didn't know how to answer the question. How was Noelle? Beanie wasn't sure even though he'd visited her thirty minutes ago at the St. Killian police department where she remained behind bars, accused of murdering her co-worker, Eamon Taylor.

Separated from his wife by a thick partition of bullet-proof Plexiglas, Beanie had struggled to contain his frustration and anger. The idea of his wife in jail for a crime he knew she could never commit sent his blood pressure soaring. Beanie feared he might have a stroke if he didn't calm down.

Noelle's voice through the telephone had been weary, but resilient. His wife was tenacious and strong, but he feared the confidence she'd projected was for his benefit. She didn't want him to worry or be afraid, but how could he not. Noelle hadn't looked completely broken, but Beanie could tell she was still just as shell-shocked and confused by her arrest as he was.

"I guess you guys heard what happened," Beanie said, sinking into his chair, resisting the urge to drop his head on the desk and pound his fists against the scarred wood.

"Burt Bronson told us," said Sophie taking the seat in front of his desk.

When the shock and horror of Noelle's arrest had subsided to the point where Beanie felt he was able to function, if not normally, then good enough to make phone calls, one of the people he'd contacted was the *Palmchat Gazette's* publisher. Despite his normally gruff demeanor, Burt had been compassionate and understanding, offering his assistance and encouraging Beanie to take the time he needed to support his wife and family.

Beanie had been grateful for the paid leave, especially when he'd been informed that Noelle's bail hearing wouldn't take place for another three days. He hated the thought of Noelle having to sit in jail while waiting to get out of jail. Fearful of Noelle being abused or mistreated while incarcerated made sleep impossible.

"Noelle is ... hanging in there as much as possible," said Beanie, staring at the photo prominently displayed in a fancy, brushed silver frame—he and Noelle on their wedding day, a glorious and beautiful occasion. Beanie still couldn't believe he'd been lucky enough to marry the girl of his dreams.

Before meeting Noelle, he'd never given much thought to happily ever after and didn't consider himself a very romantic guy. However, the day he'd met her, he'd known she was the kind of woman to fall in love with, a woman he could give his heart to, a true soul mate in every sense of the word. A lover and best friend worthy of his devotion, protection, and affection.

Leaving Noelle behind at the St. Killian police department had nearly killed Beanie, but he refused to fall apart.

More than ever before, the love of his life needed him. Beanie planned to move heaven and earth, if need be, to make sure his wife beat the bogus charges against her.

"How are the boys?" Caleb asked.

"They're fine. Noelle's mom is keeping them," said Beanie. "They love their grandma. I told Ethan that mommy had to take a trip, but she'll be back soon. I'm just thankful the boys are not old enough to understand the truth because I don't think I could tell them ..."

How could he tell the boys that mommy was in jail when he could hardly believe it himself?

"Well, even if they were old enough to understand, they wouldn't find out from the *Palmchat Gazette*," said Sophie, with her patented sassy defiance. "Caleb talked to Leo, and he agreed that the newspaper is not going to mention the name of the alleged suspect in Eamon Taylor's murder."

"We told that Leo Bronson we would strike if he insisted on naming Noelle as the suspect in custody," said Caleb, full of the righteous indignation he was known for. "He tried to give us the public has the right to know bullshit, but we shut him down quick."

"He didn't want another potential mutiny," said Stevie.

Beanie chuckled a bit, remembering the day when Leo Bronson had bled red ink over all their articles, and the staff had threatened to quit. How many days ago had that been? Beanie wasn't sure, and it didn't matter anymore.

"Have you hired a lawyer?" Sophie asked.

Beanie shook his head. "I've spent the last two days trying to gather as much money as possible for Noelle's bail, which I'm figuring will be astronomical, considering the charges."

"You should call Attorney Octavia Constant," said Sophie. "She's excellent, trust me."

Caleb nodded. "She's known for getting people released on their own recognizance."

"Even murderers," Stevie chimed in.

"Stevie ..." Sophie chided, scowling at the paper's resident slacker.

"Sorry." Stevie apologized, immediately contrite. "I didn't mean to suggest that Noelle is a murderer because she obviously isn't, I was just—"

"It's okay, man," said Beanie. "I knew what you meant."

Caleb said, "I was assigned the story, and I talked to Officer Fields, but all he would tell me is that the evidence against Noelle is solid, which I find hard to believe. Noelle would never hurt anyone."

"Off the record?" Beanie asked though he knew Caleb would never publish their private conversation.

"Absolutely," said Caleb.

"Nobody is thinking about selling papers right now," said Sophie. "We all know Noelle is innocent. We just want to help you clear her name if we can."

"But, we have to know what we're up against so we can figure out where to start," said Stevie.

Touched by his friends' willingness to lay aside ambition to help him, Beanie said, "The evidence is worse than solid. It's positively incriminating. If Noelle weren't my wife, I would absolutely believe that she'd killed Eamon Taylor."

Chapter Twenty

Chopped into pieces, the bloody corpse had been placed on a sheet of plastic in the trunk.

The arms and legs had been sawed from the torso. The head, a crushed mess of bloody pulp and bone, had been severed from the neck.

Interesting that you find it disturbing ... considering that this is your gruesome handiwork, Dr. Bean.

That's not true!

Isn't it, though? Let's not waste time with pretense, Dr. Bean. You and I both know that you killed Eamon Taylor. You bashed his head in with a shovel, and then you cut his body up and—

Noelle opened her eyes and sat up on the cot bolted to the wall in the holding cell, her home for the past two days. Dressed in drab prison garb, she rubbed her arms as she stared around the cell. No bigger than a closet, there was barely enough space for the cot, the toilet, and the sink. Glancing right, she gazed at the bars denying her freedom.

Was this real? Was this her life? Was she really in jail? Had she been accused of committing a gruesome, heinous crime? How had this happened to her?

Flashing back to the day of her arrest, Noelle wondered if what had happened to her had been a nightmare or some form of insanity. When Detective Janvier had requested to question her alone, she never in a million lifetimes could have imagined why he'd wanted to interrogate her privately.

Noelle had been wary of speaking with the detective without Beanie, but when Janvier mentioned Eamon, she'd panicked. Thinking that somehow the stolen car was connected to Eamon's harassment claims, Noelle agreed to Janvier's request because she didn't want Beanie to learn the truth from anyone except her.

In the frigid interrogation room, Noelle quickly realized she hadn't been summoned to the police station because of her stolen car.

"Dr. Bean, I asked you about Eamon Taylor because I wanted to confirm your knowledge of and connection to him," Detective Janvier had begun. Sitting across from her, a blue file between them on the cold steel table, he was probing and yet hesitant. She couldn't tell if his Inspector Clouseau routine was real or not. Was he really jumpy and befuddled? Or did he want her to think he wasn't as smart or sharp as he really was, for some reason?

"I know Eamon Taylor," she'd admitted. "He works with me at the Palmchat Pharmacy. He's the assistant pharmacist."

Nodding, Janvier asked, "And can you please describe your working relationship?"

"What do you mean describe it?"

"Do the two of you work well together?" asked Janvier. "Do you get along? Do you like each other?"

Wary of the direction of the conversation, Noelle said, "We have a professional relationship."

"So there is no conflict or hostility between the two of you?"

At that moment, Noelle had been convinced Eamon had filed a criminal complaint against her.

She had been wrong.

"Detective, what are these questions about?" Noelle had asked. "I don't understand—"

"Neither do I," interrupted Janvier. "So I am hoping you can explain some things to me. Specifically, I would like to know why you bludgeoned Eamon Taylor to death with a shovel and then hacked his body into several pieces which you then put in the trunk of a car which you claimed was stolen."

There had been no way for Noelle to explain because she'd momentarily lost the ability to speak. All cognitive function had ceased.

Noelle hardly remembered the rest of the interrogation.

It was all a blur of Janvier's accusations and her denials until he'd opened the blue folder and pulled out the photos of Eamon's desecrated corpse. Close-up shots of bloody body parts and then a photo of a shovel, the blade crusted with desiccated human remains.

Noelle had almost vomited.

She'd recognized the shovel. Staring at the bent shovel head, Noelle had remembered the day she'd haggled with the owner of the small hardware store. The shovel used to kill Eamon belonged to her and had her fingerprints all over it.

"You are familiar with that shovel?" asked Janvier.

"It was stolen ..." Noelle whispered, dizzy with confusion and disbelief. "Someone stole it."

"Someone stole the shovel?"

Looking up from the horrific photos, Noelle said, "That shovel was stolen from my shed."

"So it is your shovel," said Janvier, a smug smirk playing at the corners of his mouth.

"The person who stole the shovel must have killed Eamon because—"

"When did the alleged theft of the shovel occur?"

Noelle struggled to think. "A week ago, maybe. I discovered—"

"And did you report this theft?"

Shaking her head, Noelle said, "I didn't because I only paid half price for it and I just thought—"

"I don't need to hear anymore, Dr. Bean," Janvier had announced. "I'm placing you under arrest for the murder of Eamon Taylor."

Noelle shuddered, remembering the detective's cruel, confusing words.

She couldn't believe she'd been arrested for killing Eamon. She couldn't believe Eamon was dead. It sickened and saddened her to think of him meeting such a violent, vicious end.

Noelle lay on the cot, curled into a ball, and faced the wall.

Only one more day to her bail hearing. She would make it because she had to. She couldn't fall apart or unravel at the seams. She had to get the charges against her dropped. She had to prove she was innocent. As soon as she was out of jail, she would hire a lawyer and explain her side of this tragedy.

Despite the confrontation she'd had with Eamon and the deterioration of their working relationship, she hadn't killed him. Maybe part of her had hated him for levying false accusations of harassment against her, but she'd wanted to resolve things quickly and quietly. She wanted Eamon Taylor out of her life, but she hadn't wanted him dead.

Weary and exhausted, Noelle doubted she would be able to sleep. Each time she closed her eyes, gruesome images flooded her mind. The photos Detective Janvier had forced her to stare at were burned into her brain. Nothing could blot them out. Not thoughts of Beanie or memories of the boys. Whenever she reflected on her family, the grisly photos of Eamon's hacked remains invaded her mind.

"Hey, Nobody ..." A whispered voice floated into the cell, paralyzing Noelle for a moment.

Noelle sat up and jumped off her cot.

Heart thundering, she stared at the officer standing outside the bars of her cell. He was tall and gangly with a toffee-colored complexion and a furtive gaze. Despite his uniform, he had a distinct Handweg swagger she recognized and figured his decision to protect and serve hadn't been completely altruistic.

What terrorized her, even more, was his use of her former street name—Nobody.

"My name is Dr. Noelle Bean," she said. "I don't—"

"Shut the fuck up and listen." He beckoned for her to come closer.

Defiant, Noelle shook her head, determined not to be intimidated.

"Don't make me come inside that cell, bitch," he threatened. "I said come closer."

Worried, Noelle nevertheless took her time as she approached him. "What do you—"

His hand snaked through the bars, clamped around her throat and yanked her against the cold steel rods.

"Don't scream and don't move," he said, voice low and gruff. "I'll break your fucking neck and then make it look like you hung yourself in your cell. You understand me?"

Trembling and crying, and with her face smashed against the bars of her cell, Noelle managed to nod.

"So a mutual friend of ours is offering you a deal," he said. "If you take the deal, this friend of ours will make all your problems go away. These bullshit charges against you will be dropped. So, Dr. Bean, what should I tell our friend?"

The officer released her. Noelle stumbled, grabbing the bars with one hand to steady herself and using the other to swipe her tears away. She knew exactly who the "mutual friend" was and she understood the deal he was offering her.

Grady Palmer was offering to get the murder charges against her dropped, and all she had to do was help the bastard start an illegal pill farm.

"I ain't got all fucking day, bitch," the officer said. "What do I tell our friend? You taking the deal?"

Glaring at the officer, a PC-5 plant, she realized, Noelle smiled and said, "You tell Grady Palmer to kiss my ass."

Chapter Twenty-One

"So, I know you're anxious to get home and hug your little boys," said Octavia Constant as she took a seat on the tufted couch in the living area of a plush suite at the Queen Palm hotel. "But I need to discuss a few things with you about the case."

Noelle was relieved the successful defense attorney had agreed to represent her. Yesterday, Beanie had contacted Octavia to retain her services. A referral from Beanie's co-worker Sophie Carter helped to persuade Octavia to take her case.

This morning, Octavia had arrived in St. Killian on the first flight from St. Mateo where she was based. Beanie picked her up from the airport and drove her to the courthouse for Noelle's nine a.m. bail hearing. Noelle had liked Octavia the moment she'd met her. Petite and no-nonsense, Octavia was smart, accomplished and determined, qualities Noelle had cultivated in her own life and tried her best to project.

Sitting next to Beanie, Noelle nodded. "Of course. And I want to thank you again for getting me released on my own recognizance."

"Actually, that was all you," said Octavia, smiling. "Your ties to the community and your lack of criminal history convinced the judge that you weren't a flight risk despite the seriousness of your charges."

"Speaking of the charges," said Beanie. "How are we going to get them dropped?"

"Do I really have a chance to beat these charges?" Noelle asked, trying to prepare herself for a worst-case scenario. "The evidence is pretty damaging."

"The evidence against you is damning, actually," Octavia admitted. "Between the shovel with your fingerprints all over it and the dead body in the trunk of your car, it does look worse than bad."

Noelle nodded slowly, and as Beanie squeezed her hand, she tried to draw comfort from his gesture, but all she could think was that her life would be over if she were convicted of a crime she hadn't committed. Being separated from Beanie and the boys would kill her.

"However, looks can be, and often are, deceiving," Octavia said. "My job is to expose the deception. I'm also very good at discovering what I call the better suspect. That is, someone who had a much better motive than you did to murder the victim."

"But, I don't have a motive," Noelle insisted. "I didn't want Eamon dead."

"Your working relationship wasn't so great, though," said Octavia, giving Noelle a shrewd look.

"Noelle didn't have any beef with Eamon Taylor," Beanie said, disputing Octavia's claim.

"You and Eamon Taylor had a big argument at the pharmacy a few days before he was killed," Octavia said.

Beanie turned to her. "Is that true?"

Noelle cleared her throat, panicked. Just how much did her lawyer know about the conflict with Eamon, she wondered. "Well ..."

"Apparently, the police talked to some of your co-workers at the pharmacy," said Octavia. "These co-workers told the cops that you and Eamon had a huge argument. They weren't sure what the argument was about, but they remembered that you threatened Eamon. You said something about burying him in a grave."

Beanie stared at her. "Noelle, is that true?"

Exhaling, Noelle stood, walked to a desk in the corner and then faced her husband and her attorney, both of whom were waiting for her to explain herself.

"It was just a misunderstanding," said Noelle, knowing she should be completely honest, especially with her attorney, and not omit important facts that could potentially help Octavia represent her. "I got frustrated with him, and I said some things that were very unprofessional and which I regret, but ... I didn't want to kill him."

"Of course, you didn't, babe," said Beanie. "You could never hurt anybody."

"But, the argument between you and Eamon could be problematic," said Octavia. "I'm also concerned because you don't have an alibi for the murder. The police have an estimated time of death for Eamon Taylor, and it's one of the days when you were off from work."

"I spent those days with my boys," Noelle said, returning to her seat next to Beanie.

"A three-year-old and a ten-month-old can't testify on their mother's behalf," said Octavia. "But, we'll deal with that. What I plan to start focusing on is getting the evidence against you ruled as inadmissible considering that the body and the shovel were found in a stolen car."

"My stolen car," said Noelle.

"Which the police don't think was actually stolen," said Octavia.

"Are you serious?" Beanie demanded. "The cops think Noelle lied about being carjacked?"

Nodding, Octavia said, "The police believe Noelle fabricated the story so that if the car was found, she would be able to claim she had nothing to do with the body in the trunk because the car had been stolen. Similarly, they don't believe your story about the stolen shovel, either."

"Oh God ..." Noelle breathed, dragging her hands down her face, determined not to cry.

"Babe, it's going to be okay." Beanie put an arm around her, pulled her close to him, and kissed her forehead.

"Beanie's right," Octavia said. "What concerns me is what the police don't believe: that both your car and your shovel were stolen and then these items end up as the most damaging evidence in a murder investigation."

"Someone is trying to set me up," Noelle said. "They want it to look like I killed Eamon, but I didn't. I wouldn't have killed him. I couldn't have."

Nodding, Octavia said, "I have to say I agree. It does appear that someone is trying to make you look guilty. But, it's a very serious claim and one that, historically, jurors don't really believe. Not unless there's a confession from the real killer."

"Who would want to make Noelle look guilty?" Beanie asked.

"That's a lot of trouble for someone to go through," Octavia said. "Whoever it is would really have to hate you, Noelle."

"Helen Farber hates me," Noelle said, staring at her trembling hands.

"Who is Helen Farber?" Octavia asked.

"She used to work at the pharmacy with Noelle," Beanie answered. "Babe, you really think Helen would kill a guy and set you up for the murder?"

"Look, all I know is Helen Farber hates me, okay," Noelle said, fatigue and frustration wearing her down.

"Why does this Helen Farber hate you?" asked Octavia.

"She was fired from the pharmacy for stealing pain meds," said Noelle. "I found out about it, and I notified the company. She was coming to work high, and she was making mistakes. I only told upper management because I was trying to protect our customers, but Helen thought I back-stabbed her by ratting on her because I wanted her job."

"So you think Helen Farber wanted revenge on you?" Octavia asked.

"I know she did," said Noelle. "I saw her recently."

"When?" Beanie asked.

"After one of my lectures at the university," Noelle said. "I didn't tell you about it because I didn't think it was a big deal. Helen got in my face, claiming I ruined her life but I thought she was bitter. But, she told me that one day someone would ruin my life as I'd ruined hers. She said karma was a bitch, and so was she."

"That sounds like a definite threat against Noelle."

"Possibly," said Octavia, a bit more circumspect. "Or, maybe a disgruntled woman seizing the opportunity to give her foe a piece of her mind. Nevertheless, I'll look into it. My cousin Icarus is flying in tomorrow to help with some investigating. I'll have him check out Helen Farber, but I really want more insight into Eamon Taylor."

"You want to find the better suspect," said Beanie. "I think that's a good idea. Eamon Taylor is from Handweg Gardens. It's a tough part of the island."

"You grew up there, too, right Noelle?" Octavia tilted her head, giving Noelle a shrewd glance.

Noelle nodded. "Yeah, I grew up there," she said, wanting to hide the fact and yet feeling ashamed for wishing she had been born anywhere else.

"But, Noelle left there a long time ago," said Beanie, a hint of pride in his voice, as though her escape from Handweg meant she no longer carried the stigma of being from the hood and thus was more acceptable.

Octavia said, "Well, I have been thinking about how Eamon was killed, and it feels very personal to me."

"Personal?" Noelle asked.

"The violence of it," she said. "Crushing his skull with a shovel is excessive and angry. I know we've said that someone is trying to make you look guilty, and I think that's true, but ... "

Beanie asked, "But, what?"

Octavia glanced at Noelle and Beanie. "So, our theory is that someone killed Eamon to set Noelle up for a murder. That means someone wants revenge on you, Noelle. So, they decided to make you look like a cold-blooded killer. But, it also means it doesn't matter who they kill. That person could have killed anyone and then set it up to make Noelle look guilty."

"That's true," said Beanie.

"You don't think that anymore?" Noelle asked, her apprehension growing.

"I'm wondering if someone wanted Eamon dead," said Octavia. "Maybe this is not about revenge on Noelle. Maybe someone wanted to kill Eamon Taylor, and Noelle is just a convenient scapegoat."

Chapter Twenty-Two

"I can't believe that crazy bitch Helen set you up," Beanie said, and then sighed, dragging a hand along his jaw.

"Maybe she didn't set me up," said Noelle, staring across the kitchen table at her loving, devoted husband. A compassionate man who deserved better than a wife keeping secrets from him.

Noelle took a deep breath. She wasn't in the mood for true confessions, but the boys were asleep now, and there was secret she'd realized she needed to share with Beanie, one she couldn't put off telling him any longer.

A secret she shouldn't have kept from him.

After leaving Octavia's office, she and Beanie had picked up the boys from her mother's house.

Seeing Ethan and Evan for the first time in three days had instantly healed her broken heart. She hadn't been able to stop holding them, crying tears of joy as she kissed their beautiful little faces and promised never to leave them again. Determined to make things seem as normal as possible, they took the boys to a local park where they'd spent almost three hours enjoying time together.

For the boys' sake, Noelle forced herself to project a happy, carefree attitude. She didn't want the boys to pick up on the fear and panic washing over her. She tried to ignore the voices in her mind, whispering to her, telling her to enjoy the time while she could because soon she'd be locked up and unable to push Ethan on the swings or watch Evan try to crawl across a blanket.

"Then who the hell is framing you?" Beanie threw up his hands in frustration. "You don't have any enemies except Helen."

"So, you think Helen stole my shovel?"

"She could have," Beanie said. "Helen knows where we live. She probably knew she would need to kill Eamon with some object that belonged to you. So, she broke into our house, found the shovel in the shed and took it. She probably figured you had used it so, of course, it would have your fingerprints on it."

"But what if my fingerprints hadn't been on the shovel?" Noelle asked. "What if you had used the shovel? Then her plan to get revenge on me would have gone completely left because you would have been accused of killing Eamon."

"She might have considered that, actually," said Beanie. "If her ultimate goal is to ruin your life then she accomplishes that if your husband is thrown in jail for murder."

Noelle nodded. "Any separation of our family would devastate me."

"Doesn't matter which one of us goes down for Eamon's murder," Beanie said. "Helen wins as long as one of us ends up in prison for the rest of our lives."

"But what about my car?" Noelle asked. "Helen didn't carjack me. It was some guy wearing a mask like in that horror movie."

"*Friday the 13th*?"

Shaking her head, Noelle said, "No, the other one. *Halloween.*"

Beanie shrugged. "Maybe she paid someone to steal your car."

"Maybe, but ..." Noelle rubbed her eyes. "I just can't see Helen hitting Eamon in the head with a shovel."

"Elle, why does it sound like you don't think Helen framed you?"

"I don't know," said Noelle, looking away for a second and then back at Beanie. "Maybe because ... Beanie, there's something I need to tell you. Something I didn't tell Octavia."

"Babe, you have to tell your lawyer everything."

"I know that," said Noelle. "And I will tell her, but I wanted to tell you first."

Beanie took her hand and then looked at her, waiting.

"A few weeks ago," Noelle said, "I was approached by someone who wanted me to participate in a criminal activity which would involve the pharmacy."

"Noelle, start from the beginning and tell me everything."

Noelle stared at their intertwined fingers, knowing she couldn't tell him everything about Grady Palmer's indecent proposal. She would tell him as much as she could without revealing the truth about the past of violence and mayhem she'd overcome but was too ashamed to reveal to Beanie. Lying was selfish and violated the vows she'd promised to cherish and keep, but she couldn't risk losing Beanie, not now, when she needed him the most when her freedom and her life as she knew it was at stake.

"So this Grady Palmer asshole is PC-5?" Beanie asked once she'd finished. His voice was curt, betraying his anger but she could tell he was trying not to lose control of his temper.

"That's what he told me," she said, which was true. When they'd first met fifteen years ago, Grady had told her about his affiliation with the island gang.

"Why did he approach you?"

"He knows I'm from Handweg," said Noelle. "That's not a secret. I guess he thinks because we're from the same neighborhood that I would be more agreeable to his request, but I told him, several times, to go to hell."

"And I guess then he threatened you?"

Noelle hesitated as Beanie's rage increased. "Yes, he threatened me, but—"

Beanie exploded, just as she'd expected he would. Cursing, he jumped up from the table and paced in front of the sink. Jaws clenched, he slammed his fist into his palm as he vowed to kill Grady Palmer.

"You can't go after him," Noelle warned.

"The son of a bitch threatened you," said Beanie. "I'm not letting him get away with that."

"Beanie, please, calm down and listen to me, okay?" Noelle stood, walked to Beanie and grabbed his hands, forcing his fists apart. "There's something else you need to know."

His expression wary, Beanie stared at her.

After clearing her throat, Noelle said, "I think the PC-5 killed Eamon to force me to work for them."

Beanie's wariness gave way to confusion. "What?"

Following some stammering reluctance, Noelle told Beanie about the guard and Grady's deal.

Beanie frowned, his expression incredulous. "So, they set you up for murder and then they'll get the charges dropped if you help with the pill farm?"

Part of Noelle shared her husband's disbelief. It didn't seem like the PC-5's style to perpetrate a frame job to force her hand. The PC-5 she remembered was all about brute force intimidation, but she'd been out of that life for fifteen years. The gang might have changed their tactics as leadership changed.

Noelle said, "And if I refuse, they let me go to prison for a crime I didn't commit."

Beanie shook his head. "That's not going to happen."

"No, it's not," Noelle said. "I'm going to prove the PC-5 is setting me up and I'll need your help.

Guiding him back to the table, Noelle told him to sit, and she sank into the chair across from him. Reaching across the table, she grabbed his hands. Beanie listened to her plan without comment. Wary of his silence, Noelle asked, "What do you think? Is it a crazy idea? Can it work?"

"Well, it's so crazy it just might work, but—"

"It has to work," Noelle said. "If it doesn't, then ..."

Beanie said, "I'll start getting together everything I think we'll need."

Encouraged by his endorsement of her idea, Noelle said, "Beanie ..."

Beanie reached across the table and took her hand.

Noelle asked, "You believe me, right?"

"What do you mean?"

"You don't believe I killed Eamon Taylor, do you?"

Beanie frowned. "Dr. Noelle Chartres Bean. Did you really just ask me that? How could you think that I would ever think you could kill someone—"

"But the evidence is—"

"I don't give a damn about the evidence," Beanie said. "Look, even if you confessed to me right now that you killed Eamon Taylor, I wouldn't believe you because I know you. You could never hurt anyone."

Tears pricked Noelle's eyes. The love and compassion in his luminous brown eyes was so sincere, she felt it in the core of her soul ... and yet she knew she didn't deserve his heartfelt sentiment because she was keeping so many secrets from him ... but the truth might rip them apart, something she couldn't bear.

"I know you would never hurt anyone," said Beanie.

"Even though I'm from Handweg," Noelle said.

"Yeah, but you're different," said Beanie. "You didn't let that bad environment turn you into one of those Handweg Ho girls."

Something hard dropped into her stomach as her heart raced.

She should be honest with Beanie. His perception of her was completely wrong. The moment of honesty was upon her, bearing down like the heaviest, most oppressive weight. She should come clean with Beanie. Tell him everything he didn't know about her. Tell him the things he could never imagine. The things he might not accept.

Beanie stood. "I'm going to call Stevie Bishop. I think he can help with some of the things we need."

Nodding, Noelle watched Beanie leave the kitchen.

The moment of honesty trailed behind him, leaving increased guilt in its wake, but she resolved to ignore it. She would have to find a way to deal with the guilty feelings. Beanie couldn't know the truth about her. If he ever found out about the awful things she'd done, he would be convinced that she was absolutely capable of murder.

Chapter Twenty-Three

"Okay, Octavia, thanks for calling," said Noelle, her heart sinking, trying not to cry as she listened to the woman's words of encouragement and determination. "Okay, I will. Talk to you soon."

A few feet away, Beanie stood near the T.V. armoire in the living room, watching her intently, waiting for her to hang up the phone and relay the news her lawyer had called to give them.

Reluctant to share grim tidings, Noelle replaced the cordless receiver in its base on the end table and took a deep breath as she faced Beanie.

"What's the matter?" Beanie walked toward her, his face a mirror of the emotions she couldn't contain. "What did Octavia say?"

"Wasn't good news," Noelle said, slowly sinking down onto the couch.

Beanie sat next to her. "Tell me."

Shaking her head, Noelle said, "Helen Farber couldn't have killed Eamon to frame me. Octavia found out that Helen has an airtight alibi for the day of Eamon's murder."

Beanie exhaled. "Is Octavia sure?"

Noelle nodded, wringing her hands. "Apparently, the day Helen confronted me after my lecture at the university, she went on a bender and overdosed. A security guard found her passed out in her car in the faculty parking lot. The next day, her family took her to the Aerie Islands where she was checked into the Rakestraw-Blake Center, which has a 90-day drug treatment program."

"The day after that lecture," said Beanie. "That's more than a month ago."

"Which means Helen didn't kill Eamon and frame me for his murder," Noelle said. "As upset as I am, I had a feeling Helen hadn't done it."

"It's got to be the PC-5," said Beanie. "Grady Palmer."

"That's what I have to prove," Noelle said. "Speaking of that, is Stevie Bishop going to be able to help us?"

"He said he's got exactly what we need," Beanie said. "I'm going to talk to him at work today. Speaking of that, I need to get going."

"I'm going to get the boys ready to drop off at my mom's," Noelle said, standing.

Beanie stood and pulled her into his arms. "Let's meet for lunch, okay? Around one o'clock. We can work out the details of your plan."

Noelle stood on her toes to kiss him.

"Don't worry, Elle," he said, wrapping her in his strong arms. "Everything is going to be okay. Trust me. I will not let you go to jail for something you didn't do."

After Beanie left for work, Noelle hustled the boys into the car and took them to her mother's house in Handweg Gardens. While the boys played with the dogs in the backyard, Noelle and her mom sat in the kitchen and discussed her terrible ordeal. After hours of tears, prayers, and words of encouragement from her mother, Noelle left to pick Beanie up from the newspaper, and they went to a park near the marina for lunch.

It was a gorgeous afternoon. Ocean breezes, sun dancing on the water and dancing off the chrome of boats parked in slips along the dock ...

Noelle had grabbed salads and sandwiches from a popular local deli before she picked up Beanie from the *Palmchat Gazette* offices. At the park across from the marina, she and Beanie found a bench beneath a tall Queen Palm for their working lunch.

"Okay, let's go over the plan again," Beanie said after they'd finished eating.

Noelle sighed. "Roland, we have gone over the plan a dozen times already."

Beanie said, "And we'll go over it a dozen more until I'm convinced that nothing can go wrong."

Using the empty paper bag as a makeshift trash receptacle for their food wrappers and used napkins, Noelle said, "I really don't think—"

Beanie rubbed his chin. "Humor me, Elle. Please."

Sighing, Noelle said, "Okay, I'm going to text Grady Palmer and request a meeting with him. During the meeting, I will agree to work for him if he will admit to having Eamon Taylor killed so he could frame me. I will be making an audiovisual recording while wearing a covert spy camera which looks like a watch."

"Stevie's going to give me the watch later today," said Beanie. "He's going to show me how to use it, and I'll show you. We'll practice with the watch until you're comfortable operating it."

Noelle went on. "While I'm getting Grady Palmer on tape incriminating himself, you'll be in the car watching and waiting."

"If anything goes wrong," Beanie said, "I'll be there."

"If anything goes wrong," Noelle said, "They'll ..."

Looking away, Noelle stared at the boats, bobbing gently in the buoyant aqua water. She couldn't bring herself to finish the sentence. Things going wrong meant Grady Palmer had figured out she was wearing undercover surveillance. If that happened, Grady would kill her.

"The PC-5 is not going to hurt you," Beanie said, caressing her cheek as he gazed at her. "I won't let them. I promise."

"I know," she said, though she hated putting Beanie in the position of having to defend her against a ruthless bastard who wouldn't think twice about killing him.

"So, you have a way to get in touch with Grady Palmer, right?"

"Some way, he found my phone number and sent me a text," she said. "So, I can text him."

"Might as well do it now," Beanie said.

"Before I do," Noelle said, staring at the blades of grass surrounding her toes. "There's something I need to tell you."

"Not more bad news," said Beanie, lifting her chin.

"Something you should know," she said, gazing at him. "Something I should have told you about Eamon Taylor."

Beanie frowned. "What about him?"

"It's about the argument I had with him," Noelle said.

"The argument your co-workers told the cops about," said Beanie.

"The argument we had could cause problems for me," Noelle said, reaching for Beanie's hand. "If the cops find out what Eamon and I were arguing about, they might think that the reason behind the argument is my motive for killing Eamon."

"Babe, what do you mean?" Beanie took both of her hands in his. "What were you arguing about?"

"Eamon Taylor was trying to ruin my career and my reputation and everything I'd worked for," she said, determined to continue despite the apprehension in Beanie's stare. "I told Eamon that if he tried to dig a grave for me, I would bury him in it."

"Why would you say that to him?"

After a deep breath, Noelle said, "Because Eamon Taylor accused me of sexually harassing him."

Chapter Twenty-Four

Beanie stared at his blank computer screen. All morning, he'd been working on his latest story. He had all his facts. He had all the quotes he needed. He knew how he wanted to present the information to his readers. Still, the damn words wouldn't come, and he was on a deadline.

Exhaling, Beanie rubbed his eyes.

He knew why he was distracted.

Noelle's bombshell about Eamon's sexual harassment claim had rattled him. Yesterday, when she'd told him, Beanie hadn't known what to think or say. His silence had worried Noelle, made her think he was suspicious of her, but he was quick to assure her that he was just beyond shocked. There was no way he would ever believe his wife had sexually harassed a co-worker. It didn't make sense. Noelle had worked too hard to build her career. She would never risk her reputation to hook-up with some college kid. She would never break their wedding vows or do anything to destroy their family.

The Dr. Noelle Chartres Bean he knew could never do anything so … ridiculously uncharacteristic.

And yet, Beanie couldn't ignore the crazy thoughts forcing him to wonder if the harassment claims could be true. Beanie had met Eamon once, at a dinner the pharmacy had given for the interns. Eamon Taylor was a good-looking guy. He was charismatic with good conversation skills. Eamon and Noelle seemed to have a friendly, casual relationship but Beanie didn't remember witnessing anything inappropriate in their interactions. He hadn't seen any suspicious behavior. No longing glances or secret gazes between them.

Noelle had sworn the sexual harassment claims were false. She'd promised him that Eamon was lying. Beanie didn't doubt her—or, did he? Noelle had been keeping things from him. Important things like Grady Palmer. If she wasn't facing this murder charge, would she have told him about the PC-5 thug's proposition?

Beanie glanced at the photo of Noelle on his desk. He didn't want to question their marriage. He didn't want to wonder if his marriage was as solid as he assumed but the questions were in his head, undeniable and unavoidable. What the hell else was Noelle keeping from him?

Beanie rubbed his jaw.

If Noelle was keeping secrets, it meant she didn't trust him and if she didn't trust him, then ... Beanie didn't want to think about it. Noelle probably hadn't wanted to worry him. He understood that. He didn't like it. He wished she would have told him about that PC-5 thug as soon as the bastard had propositioned her, but ...

There was something else Beanie didn't want to question. Noelle's innocence. *I told Eamon that if he tried to dig a grave for me, I would bury him in it.* Was it possible that Noelle had ... ?

Beanie couldn't finish the thought. He felt traitorous even thinking his wife could be capable of what the police had accused her of doing. There was no way Noelle could have bashed Eamon Taylor's head in with a shovel.

You don't believe I killed Eamon Taylor, do you?

Beanie would never believe Noelle had anything to do with Eamon's death. He didn't care about the shovel with her prints on it or the body found in the trunk of her car, or—

"Beanie, I gotta show you something ..."

Beanie glanced up. Sophie Carter dropped down in the chair in front of his old battered desk. Her face alive and animated, she pushed a piece of paper across the scarred surface.

"What is this?" Beanie stared at the print-out of an email.

"Anonymous tip," said Sophie, dark brown eyes dancing with excitement and intrigue. "It was just emailed to me a few minutes ago. You gotta read it."

Pushing away the worries about Noelle and Eamon, Beanie picked up the email and stared at it.

The cops have the wrong suspect for murder of Eamon Taylor.
Check out Kevin Cook.
He hated Eamon and wanted him dead.

Chapter Twenty-Five

A trip to the grocery store was the last thing Noelle wanted to tackle, even without a rambunctious three-year-old and a fussy, teething ten-month-old to contend with, but she had to.

After Beanie left for work, she'd gotten Ethan and Evan fed, bathed and dressed and then dropped them off at her mom's house. Without the boys, she could get her To Do list taken care of quickly, but she missed Ethan and Evan. She wondered if she should spend every moment she could with them while she still could, while she was still free.

Noelle pushed the shopping cart through the fresh produce section. She shouldn't think of going to jail for a crime she hadn't committed. She wanted to be positive and hopeful, but it was becoming harder to keep a positive attitude—especially about her job.

The day after she'd been arrested, Beanie had called the company to inform them, but they hadn't given him any indication of whether or not she would be fired.

An early morning phone call from Octavia had shed more light on the situation. The Palmchat Pharmacy HR department had finally made contact. Noelle had braced herself, figuring she'd been terminated, but surprisingly, Octavia had told her the company had decided to place her on administrative leave without pay pending the results of the charges against her.

She probably should have been grateful that she hadn't been fired and the company hadn't rushed to condemn her. They had every right to disassociate themselves with a suspected murderer, but they were willing to see how the situation would play out before disavowing her.

Nevertheless, it felt foreign to be shopping for toilet paper and toothpaste at ten in the morning when she should have been working. A wave of intense melancholy washed over her. Noelle gripped the handle on the cart so she wouldn't sob. Her life was going to hell, and she didn't know how to put out the flames threatening to consume her. She couldn't help but think she was being punished for past sins. Her mother encouraged her not to condemn herself, but her mother didn't know about all the horrible things she'd done, things she'd gotten away with but shouldn't have ...

As she stopped the cart in front of an apple bin, her phone beeped. A text message. Noelle's heart raced as she pulled the phone from her purse.

The message made her knees weak, filling her with relief and revulsion.

Purple Gecko. 3 pm

It was a response from Grady Palmer, and Noelle knew exactly what the message meant. Before she'd dropped the boys off, she'd sent Grady a text requesting a meeting to talk about his offer to help her. She'd hoped he would get back to her quickly but his text put fear and guilt in her.

In the plan she'd outlined to get proof that the PC-5 had framed her, Beanie would secretly accompany her to the meeting. He would be her backup, watching out for her, keeping her safe. Even as she'd explained that plan to her husband, Noelle had known she wasn't going to stick to it. She'd known she would have to talk to Grady Palmer alone. Beanie's safety and the past she had to keep secret required her to handle the situation on her own.

If Beanie went with her to talk to Grady, and she was able to get a confession, then Beanie would want to see the video. Noelle had no idea what she would have to say or do to get the truth from Grady, but she knew their meeting would expose her past. Grady would bring up her former life as Nobody, and he might even reference some of the terrible things she'd done. She couldn't risk Beanie finding out about her days as a Handweg Ho.

Noelle would not risk destroying Beanie's perceptions and beliefs about her.

Meeting Grady alone would anger Beanie, but it was for the best. If the meeting resulted in information that would exonerate her, Noelle would take the proof to Octavia and swear her lawyer to secrecy. Beanie would be too overjoyed about the charges against her being dropped to care about how she'd obtained the truth.

Noelle stared at Grady's text again. She wasn't surprised Grady wanted to meet in Handweg Gardens. It was his turf where he could control the situation. The Purple Gecko was a dump, a seedy bar, but at least it was a public place. Although, if things went left, she couldn't rely on help from any of the bar's patrons who would not be inclined to get involved in PC-5 business. Handweg had once been her turf, too, though. She'd been away a long time, but she could still hold her own.

Noelle took a deep breath and sent a response.

I'll be there

Chapter Twenty-Six

"How'd you find out where Kevin Cook lives?" Beanie asked, staring up at the large mansion framed by towering Palm trees swaying in the early afternoon breeze.

"Inductive reasoning," said Sophie with a sassy wink and a jaunty step as she headed away from Beanie's SUV and along a path toward the house.

Like most of the homes surrounding the university, it was a sprawling Colonial plantation house, one of the former homes of an early European settler who'd brought his family to the island in the early eighteenth century. Long abandoned or sold by the original descendants, the homes were often purchased by ex-pats and foreign investors who divided the once grand manors into apartments which were rented to students and university faculty members.

Falling into step with Sophie as she walked up the wide flagstone path cut between an expansive lawn dotted with Sego Palms and mango trees, Beanie said, "Hey, before we talk to Kevin Cook, remember that this is Caleb's story, okay? Whatever we find out, we need to let him know."

"Of course, we'll tell Caleb," said Sophie, rolling her eyes. "I'm not trying to poach his story. I'm trying to help you prove that Noelle didn't kill Eamon Taylor."

Humbled by Sophie's compassion, Beanie remembered why he liked Sophie—she was smart, had spunk, and she was a go-getter, eager and anxious to make things happen. She was super ambitious, as well, and he wouldn't put it past her to co-opt a story if she thought she could contribute to the success of it. Sophie wasn't diabolical, though and he didn't think she would outright steal a story.

As they approached the door, Beanie's heart jumped and sped up as the gravity of what was about to happen hit him like a punch in the gut.

Sophie was right. Talking to Kevin Cook was not about a *Palmchat Gazette* article. It was so much more than some exclusive story or a quote from an elusive source. Noelle's freedom was at stake. If Kevin Cook had killed Eamon Taylor and then set Noelle up to look like a cold-blooded murderer, Beanie had to find out. He had to ask the right questions to get Cook to confess. He wouldn't let his wife go to jail for a crime she didn't commit.

"Kevin Cook rents the attic apartment." Sophie stopped in front of the intercom system mounted on the wall near the main door.

Beanie nodded as Sophie pushed the button to buzz the attic, his pulse racing.

He'd met Kevin Cook at the same dinner where he'd first met Eamon Taylor. Beanie didn't remember the intern as being potentially inclined to murder, but why would he have? There had been no reason to think Kevin Cook could be capable of killing someone.

Sophie opened the main door. "Come on; we're in."

"We are?" Beanie asked. "I didn't hear Cook let us in."

"He didn't answer, but the door opened," said Sophie. "Somebody else probably let us in because they didn't want us pushing the buzzer over and over."

Following Sophie into the foyer, Beanie took a deep breath and tried to calm himself. When the door opened, and he was face to face with Kevin Cook, he worried he might put his hands around the little shit's throat. He cautioned himself to remember the object of the questioning. He couldn't spook Cook or make the intern suspicious although he had to assume any questions about Eamon Taylor's death might make Cook cautious and cagey. Nevertheless, Beanie had to get the guy to incriminate himself—if, of course, Cook really was guilty. As he and Sophie had discussed in the SUV on the drive to Cook's place, they had to consider that the anonymous tip might be a scam. The real killer might be trying to point the finger at Cook and away from themselves.

After taking the stairs to the third floor, they entered a small alcove which housed a spiral staircase to the attic. Climbing the steps behind Sophie, Beanie was both eager and filled with dread. Would he get the truth from Cook? Or, was the anonymous tip bogus? Maybe some lonely weirdo with nothing better to do than send them on some wild goose chase?

"Okay, like we talked about it in the car," said Sophie, "let me ask the questions."

Beanie exhaled. "Yeah, about that ..."

"Don't try to flip the script, Beanie," Sophie warned him. "I know you probably want to grab Kevin Cook and demand the truth from him, but we can't make him feel like he's going through a St. Killian Inquisition. We gotta be sly, sneaky and smart. Matter of fact, you probably shouldn't be here. If Kevin Cook killed Eamon Taylor and set up Noelle, then as soon as he sees you, he might wonder if you suspect him."

"I'm not leaving," said Beanie, crossing his arms. "Besides, if Kevin Cook is the real killer then maybe he thinks he's smarter than everybody else. Maybe he thinks I'm too dumb to suspect him. Maybe I should let him think I'm clueless."

"We'll see," Sophie said. "But, follow my lead, okay?"

Beanie had agreed to let Sophie ask the questions while he studied Kevin Cook for signs of deception: shifty eyes, stammering, fidgeting, those classic "tells" of nervousness. He wasn't sure he would be able to keep his promise.

Sophie knocked on the door, and when it opened, a familiar face stared at Beanie.

Sarah Linde, the intern who sometimes babysat the boys, looked confused as her lips curled up into a tentative smile. "Mr. Bean? How are you? What are you doing here? Do you need me to watch the boys?"

"What are you doing here?" Beanie asked. "Isn't this Kevin Cook's place?"

Nodding, Sarah said, "Sometimes I stay here with him. We're together, remember? Did you know that?"

Beanie didn't know if Noelle had mentioned Sarah's relationship with Kevin Cook, or not. What he knew, or hoped, rather, was that his cordial relationship with the babysitter would make Sarah more comfortable about opening up and being honest.

"Sarah, this is Sophie Carter," introduced Beanie. "She works with me at the *Palmchat Gazette*. Sophie, this is Sarah Linde. She babysits Ethan and Evan sometimes."

After Sophie and Sarah shook hands and exchanged polite pleasantries, Beanie asked Sarah, "Is Kevin around?"

"We were hoping to talk to him," said Sophie.

"Kevin's not here," said Sarah, leaning against the door frame. "He's at a seminar in St. Croix."

The apology in Sarah's blue eyes did nothing to relieve Beanie's raging disappointment or his suspicions. Was Sarah lying about Kevin being out of town? He didn't sense any dishonesty in her earnest gaze, but maybe she was a damn good liar. He was probably paranoid, letting frustration make him skeptical but if Sarah and Kevin were in a relationship, then Sarah might be inclined to cover for her boyfriend. Beanie would have to be sly with the questions. Maybe even more so if the babysitter was prepared to protect Kevin.

"You know when he'll be back?" Sophie asked.

"We need to talk to him," said Beanie, hoping to take advantage of his relationship with Sarah. "You have his cell phone number so we can reach him?"

"Why do you need to talk to Kevin?" Sarah asked, not quite suspicious, but close.

"I need to ask him some questions about Eamon Taylor's murder," Beanie said.

Sophie cleared her throat dramatically, letting him know she wasn't pleased with his takeover of the interrogation but Beanie didn't have time for sly, subtle questioning techniques. He wasn't in the mood to coax the truth from Sarah.

"Eamon Taylor's murder?" echoed Sarah, a stricken look on her face.

Beanie pressed her, asking, "What do you know about Eamon's death?"

"I don't know anything about it," said Sarah, flinching and stammering. "I mean, I only know what I read online and what little information the dean of our college was able to tell us, but—"

"You're sure that's all you know?" Beanie asked.

"Beanie," chided Sophie through clenched teeth.

"Why do you think I would know something?" Sarah asked. "What are you asking me? You think I killed Eamon?"

"Sarah, no, we don't think that," said Sophie. "We were just wondering—"

"Did you kill him?" Beanie blurted out.

Sarah looked as though she'd been slapped. "What? No! I would never—"

Beanie persisted. "Did Kevin Cook kill him?"

"Okay, let's just pause for a second, please," said Sophie.

Dragging his hand along his jaw, Beanie exhaled. He'd messed up. He tipped his hand too early and had been too quick to reveal their true motives. Now there was no chance Sarah would tell them anything or answer any of their questions.

If Sarah knew anything about Kevin killing Eamon, she wasn't going to tell them. Beanie wanted to kick his own ass. Why the hell had he come at Sarah with that trite bad cop attitude, barking questions and demanding answers? He shouldn't have let himself get frustrated and flustered, not when so much was at stake, not when Noelle's freedom was at risk.

"Sarah, our colleague, Caleb Olivier, was assigned the story of Eamon Taylor's death," Sophie said, her tone calm and diplomatic, "and we wanted to help him out by getting some reaction from some of Eamon Taylor's friends about his death. We decided to start with Kevin Cook but since he's not here maybe we can get your thoughts."

Arms crossed, Sarah looked skeptical, completely unconvinced.

"I need to be honest with you," said Beanie, thinking the truth might ease Sarah's burgeoning doubt of their motives. "We didn't come here to get your reaction to the death of Eamon Taylor."

Her chin lifted in defiance, Sarah said, "You came here to accuse me of killing Eamon Taylor. But I could never do something like that. I would never hurt Eamon. Why would you think that I killed him?"

"I don't think you killed him," said Beanie. "Listen, can Sophie and I come in so I can tell you why I'm really here."

After a moment of reluctance, Sarah relented, stepping back to allow them inside.

Inside Kevin Cook's attic abode, Sarah gathered up the books spread across the couch. After stacking the books on the coffee table, she extended a hand toward the couch. "Have a seat."

"It's okay," Beanie said, shaking his head. "Look, I really need to talk to Kevin about Eamon's murder."

"You really think Kevin killed Eamon?" asked Sarah, sinking down on the couch.

"Maybe," said Sophie.

"Did the cops tell you he's a suspect?" asked Sarah, looking down.

"Did the police talk to you?" Sophie asked.

"They talked to all of us who were in the pharmacy school with him," said Sarah, picking at her fingernails.

"What did the police ask you?" Sophie asked, moving to stand next to Beanie in front of the bookshelf.

Sarah sneaked a glance toward them before focusing on her nails again. Shrugging, she said, "Mostly, they wanted to know if Eamon had any enemies."

"What did you tell the cops?"

"I told them I didn't really know Eamon very well, which is true," said Sarah. "So, I told them I wouldn't know if Eamon had any enemies, but ..."

"But ..." Beanie prodded, sensing that Sarah had something to tell, but she was hesitant for some reason.

Frowning as she glanced at her nails, Sarah said, "But ... Eamon must have had enemies, though, right? Because he was murdered. And it was vicious and horrific. He was beaten to death with a shovel. It must have been so painful. I hate to think of what he went through. Whoever killed him must have hated him."

"But Eamon didn't have any enemies that you know, right?" Sophie asked.

Sarah stared at them. "That's what I told the cops."

"Did the cops ask you if you had any beef with Eamon?" Sophie asked.

"We all got that question," Sarah said. "The cops wanted to know what our relationship with Eamon was like. I told them we were just friendly classmates, but not especially close or anything."

"Did the cops ask you where you were when Eamon was killed?"

Nodding, Sarah stared at her nails again. "I was at the library with Tina and Jimmy and some other classmates studying for an exam."

"Did the police ask Kevin where he was the day Eamon was killed?" Beanie asked, growing frustrated by Sarah's increasing caginess.

"I'm sure they did," said Sarah. "I wasn't with Kevin when the cops talked to him."

"You know what Kevin told them?" Sophie asked.

"Kevin told the cops we were together the day Eamon Taylor was murdered ... but that wasn't true."

Chapter Twenty-Seven

"Dr. Bean ..."

Glancing up from the scarred table she'd been staring at in the booth where she sat, trying to be as inconspicuous as possible while waiting for Grady Palmer, Noelle glanced over her shoulder. Her heart dropped as she stared up at the two men glaring down at her.

"Come with us."

Both were large and muscular, frowning and menacing. Neither man was Grady Palmer, but she knew he'd sent them to collect her. The meeting wasn't going to take place at the Purple Gecko.

At three in the afternoon, there weren't many patrons in the bar, but the few people and the two bartenders gave her a sense of security, though it may have been false. Noelle knew Grady wouldn't try to hurt her with any witnesses around—which was why his thugs had been instructed to escort her to the real meeting spot.

Fighting dizziness, Noelle forced herself to calm down and think. So much for believing she could handle Grady Palmer by herself. She'd been away from Handweg too long. A true Handweg Ho would have anticipated and expected the change of venue. What the hell was she going to do now? Noelle felt paralyzed. She couldn't refuse to go and yet she was terrified of being taken to some place where she would be vulnerable and completely unprotected.

"Where are we going?" She asked, trying to buy time, knowing they wouldn't tell her.

"Mr. Palmer is waiting," said the guy who was just a bit bigger than the other guy. "We need to go."

Noelle hesitated, unsure of her next move. Depressed and desolate, she was torn between going through with her plan and abandoning the idea to get proof that Grady Palmer had set her up. Going with the goons was more than dangerous—it could prove deadly. Grady could be luring her into a trap. He'd always been vengeful and ruthless. He could be planning to kill her for taking her time about accepting his offer.

Refusing to go could cost her the chance to prove her innocence. Who else but Grady Palmer could have framed her? Not only did he have the resources to set her up but he had a crew at his disposal, willing and eager to do his bidding. Anyone of the thugs who reported to him could have stolen her shovel, used it to kill Eamon Taylor, and then stole her car to hide the body in the trunk.

"Are you coming, Dr. Bean?" questioned the man in dark glasses. "Or should I tell Mr. Palmer that this has all been a waste of his time?"

Grabbing her purse, Noelle slid across the cracked vinyl seat and stood. Before she could change her mind or talk herself out of what she had to do, Noelle said, "Let's go."

Chapter Twenty-Eight

Shocked and wary, Beanie stared at the babysitter.

"Are you saying that Kevin Cook lied to the cops?" He asked. "You weren't with Kevin when Eamon was killed?"

Sophie asked, "How do you know that Kevin told the cops you were together?"

"Because Kevin told me," said Sarah. "He said, I told the cops we were together when Eamon got killed so if they ask you, don't rat me out."

"And did you?" Sophie asked.

Sarah gave them a cryptic smile. "Did I rat on Kevin?"

"Did you tell the cops you and Kevin were together?"

"No, I didn't," said Sarah. "The cops didn't talk to me about Kevin."

"They didn't ask you to corroborate Kevin's story about you being his alibi?"

"Well, the thing is, the cops talked to me before they talked to Kevin and I told them I was at the library with friends," Sarah said. "So, maybe they will ask me to prove Kevin's alibi, but I won't be able to do it. I don't know where Kevin was when Eamon was killed but he sure as hell wasn't with me."

"You have any idea where Kevin was when Eamon was killed?"

Beanie asked, noting a slight change in Sarah's tone and demeanor. The sweet babysitter sounded more like a sinister woman scorned.

Shrugging, Sarah said, "Maybe he was killing Eamon."

Beanie's pulse took off. "What did you say?"

"Why would you say that?" asked Sophie.

Sarah dropped her head, as though she was ashamed. Did the babysitter regret her hasty admission? Would she expound upon it or would she take it back and claim she had just been kidding? Would she insist she should never have said something she didn't really mean? She might realize the gravity of her accusation and how it could affect her relationship with Kevin, which Beanie thought could have been one-sided, with Kevin in control, calling the shots and Sarah staying in line, or else.

"Sarah, do you think Kevin killed Eamon?" Beanie sat on the couch next to Sarah. "Because if you do—"

"Look, I don't know, okay?" Sarah jumped up. Sighing, she grabbed a hunk of her long blonde hair and slid her hand down to the ends. "It's just that I'm starting to wonder because I know that Kevin doesn't like Eamon."

"Just because Kevin doesn't like Eamon doesn't mean he killed him," said Sophie.

"It's more than just dislike," said Sarah, grabbing her hair again. "Kevin hates Eamon. You should hear how he talks about him. He calls Eamon an island thug because he's from that bad neighborhood. He says Eamon didn't deserve the Palmchat Pharmacy job and he only got it because Dr. Bean liked him, or something."

Beanie thought of Eamon's sexual harassment claim against Noelle. He knew Eamon's claims weren't true. They couldn't be. But why would Kevin think that Noelle liked Eamon? Had Kevin seen some interaction between Eamon and Noelle which led him to believe—

"And it's what I found, too," said Sarah. "I didn't want to think Kevin could do something so horrible but ..."

"What did you find?" Sophie asked.

"A few days ago, I was going to do Kevin's laundry. *Wife practicing*, my friend Tina calls it." Sarah rolled her eyes. "I found ... can I show you?"

Sophie nodded and then glanced at Beanie. Her look of shocked excitement mirrored the emotions whirling within him.

Sarah hurried to the galley kitchen and opened a door near the refrigerator. She took out a plastic laundry basket piled high with clothes. Walking back to the couch, she put the basket on the floor and sank to her knees.

"I know he hid it here because he didn't expect me to find it," said Sarah, staring at the basket of clothes. "He probably never thought I would want to do his laundry. We're together but not like that. I'm not his wife or anything."

Beanie had the feeling Sarah wanted to be Kevin's wife, but Kevin wasn't exactly enthusiastic about the idea.

"What do you want to show us?" Sophie asked, her tone gentle as she forced the babysitter to focus.

Sarah began removing clothes from the basket. Slowly at first, tentative and hesitant, she removed T-shirts, pants, and boxer shorts. A sob escaped her lips, and her shoulders trembled as she pulled the articles of clothing at a quicker pace, sometimes digging her hand down into the clothes, elbow deep, and at times barely touching the fabric as she plucked items from the basket and dropped them on the floor. With a ring of dirty clothes surrounding her, she paused before snatching a pair of jeans from the bottom of the basket.

"This," said Sarah, standing as she held the jeans in front of her. "Do you see this? Can you guess what it is?"

His heart pounding, Beanie stared at the jeans.

The bleached denim was stained with rusty smears. Beanie didn't need to guess what the stains were. He knew.

It was blood.

Chapter Twenty-Nine

"Well, well, well ... " Grady Palmer's deep, gravelly voice echoed through the cavernous space. "It seems Nobody is here."

Bristling at his use of her loathsome former nickname, Noelle braced herself.

She'd been dreading this moment as soon as she'd been shoved into the large, empty building where she'd been ordered to wait. Alone and terrified, she'd sent a quick text to her mother, telling her she might be late picking up the boys because her errands were taking a bit longer than she'd expected. Of course, her mother had understood and was happy for more time with her grandbabies which made Noelle feel horrible for lying, but she couldn't wallow in guilt.

Recalling the way she and Beanie had practiced with the watch, Noelle made sure she was able to operate it properly. Somewhat satisfied she could activate the watch without making Grady suspicious, she surveyed her surroundings. Light barely penetrated the row of small windows near the soaring ceilings, illuminating corrugated walls and a door which seemed to span the width of the building. The concrete floor beneath her was stained with large splotches of some dark liquid that had evaporated long ago.

Noelle had no idea where she'd been taken. Leaving the Purple

Gecko with Grady's thugs, she'd been guided to a black Mercedes sedan where she was put into the backseat. As the car sped off across the parking lot, heading away from the Purple Gecko, Noelle tried to see where she was being taken but it was impossible. The glass windows had been blacked out, and a partition between the front and back seats prevented her from seeing through the front windshield.

Turning, Noelle stared at Grady Palmer as he strode toward her, a quartet of PC-5 gang members trailing in his wake.

"Dr. Bean," he said, stopping a few feet from her, about arm's length. He could easily reach out and grab her by the throat if he felt it was necessary. "I must admit I was surprised to hear from you."

"Well, you said you could make all my troubles disappear if I agreed to help you," said Noelle, anxious to get on with getting the proof she needed.

"That was my offer," Grady confirmed.

"And is it still on the table?" Noelle asked, crossing her arms so that her right wrist, where she wore the watch, rested in the crook of her left elbow. The face of the watch, where the mini camera was hidden, was aimed in Grady's direction, capturing clear video and audio of him.

"You're willing to work with me?" Grady asked.

"I need my troubles to disappear," said Noelle, trying not to collapse even though her legs felt like jelly. "So, if you can really make that happen ..."

"I don't make promises that I don't keep," said Grady. "You know that."

She also knew his promises were usually gruesome threats to kill, steal, and destroy but she tried to ignore the terror racing through her.

"So, I'm curious," Noelle said, suddenly worried that maybe she hadn't set the watch correctly. What if nothing was being recorded? What if Grady confessed to framing her and she didn't record him because of some mistake she'd made? "How are you going to make my problems go away? I'm being charged with murder and the evidence against me is airtight. A jury won't even need to deliberate to convict me."

"Funny you should say that," said Grady.

"Say what?"

"That a jury will convict you."

"Grady, the cops have my fingerprints on a shovel which was used to kill Eamon Taylor," she said, praying she would come up with the right words to coax Grady into confessing that he'd framed her. "They found his body in my car."

"Yeah, a jury probably would think you killed him," said Grady. "But, lucky for you, they won't."

"What do you mean?"

"I mean that when you go on trial for the murder of this guy," said Grady, "I'll make sure the jury finds you not guilty."

"What? I don't understand."

"You need your problems to disappear? I'm gonna make it happen," he said, his expression smug. "You won't be convicted."

"Are you out of your mind? I can't go on trial for murder," Noelle said, her heart pounding, feeling as though things were unraveling. "Are you seriously saying that your idea of helping me is tampering with a jury?"

"Trust me, you will get off," he said, frowning. "You help me get my pharmacy started, and you won't end up in jail for the rest of your life."

"Why don't you admit the truth, Grady?"

"The truth?"

"You set me up," Noelle said. "You are framing me. You had Eamon Taylor killed, and you got one of your crew to plant evidence against me to put me in a position where I would have to help you set up your pill farm."

"What are you talking about, Nobody?" Grady asked. "I'm not trying to frame you. I'm trying to help you. Obviously, for whatever reason, it doesn't matter to me, you got pissed at this guy, and you forgot that you were supposed to be the kind, caring wife and mother of two, and you killed the motherfu—"

"I did not kill Eamon Taylor," Noelle insisted.

"You don't have to pretend with me," Grady said. "I know who you really are and what you're really capable of and—"

"You're wrong!" Noelle said. "I did not kill him. I could never—"

"Nobody, it's okay," said Grady, his patronizing tone placating. "I understand. You had to handle your business. I would have done the same thing if I had beef with—"

"Mr. Palmer, sir, excuse me," said one of the PC-5 hoods, holding an iPad. "I think you need to see this ..."

Confused, Noelle tried not to lose her mind as Grady turned from her to confer with his minions. As the five of them huddled together whispering furiously, heads bent toward the iPad, Noelle used their preoccupation to take several deep breaths and focus. Jumping to the worse conclusions was nearly impossible, but she had to calm down. She couldn't blow this chance to prove her innocence. Obviously, Grady wasn't just going to spill his guts. She had to trick him into admitting he'd framed her. She would have to be sly and stealth, appealing to his arrogance. If she could get him to boast about what he'd done to her, then—

"You lying, scheming bitch ..."

Noelle flinched at the raw hate in Grady's gaze as he stalked toward her.

Confused, she stammered. "W-what did—"

Grady's hand crashed against Noelle's face. The stinging blow sent her stumbling as a sharp, metallic taste spread over her tongue. Cowering, she glanced at Grady. His sudden rage confused her and yet one thing was crystal clear—she'd been a damn fool to think she could handle the situation with Grady Palmer on her own. Why had she agreed to meet him alone? Why had she agreed to leave the Purple Gecko with those Handweg Hoods?

"Should have known I couldn't trust you!" Grady thundered. "All that talk about wanting to work with me and needing my help was bullshit!"

Noelle shook her head. What the hell was happening? Her plan was falling apart right before her eyes, but why? How had she messed it all up? Why was Grady accusing her of lying? Had he found out she was trying to trick him into confessing? No one except Beanie knew about her plan, and he wouldn't have told anyone.

As she stepped back, Noelle glanced at the watch. Beanie had borrowed it from Stevie Bishop. Had Beanie told Stevie about her plan? Maybe, but Stevie wouldn't snitch to Grady Palmer or the PC-5, would he?

Desperate to calm Grady down, Noelle asked, "What are you talking about?"

Grady grabbed her forearm and yanked her toward him, gripping her so hard she thought he might break her arm.

"Let me go," Noelle said, trying to pull away as Grady glared at her. "You're hurting me!"

"You think you can get away with trying to set me up?" Grady asked, his nicotine breath slanting across her nose, nauseating her. "Don't you know that snitches get stitches, bitch!"

"What do you mean?" Noelle continued to struggle though she knew if she managed to get away, the PC-5 crew looming behind him, waiting to carry out whatever command he issued, would chase her down and drag her kicking and screaming back to Grady.

"When I told my boy Paco that you had come to your senses and was going to help us," said Grady, arm outstretched and hand locked on her neck, "he was suspicious. He told me I couldn't trust you and he was right. You're recording this conversation."

Noelle opened her mouth, but no words came out as she tried to push Grady's hand away.

"It's the watch," said the guy holding the iPad. "That's where the signal is coming from."

Grady released her neck only to grab her wrist. Frowning at the watch, he said, "This watch is some kind of ...? What?"

"It's got a tiny camera in it," said another thug. "She's been recording this entire time. Might have even been live streaming it."

Scowling, Grady yanked the watch off her wrist, dropped it onto the ground, and stomped on it.

"Bad mistake, bitch," he said, slamming his foot down on the watch over and over until it was unrecognizable. "You should have known that you couldn't play me and get away with it! And now, because of your stupid decisions, today is the day that Nobody dies ..."

Chapter Thirty

On her hands and knees, staring up into Grady's cold, menacing gaze, Noelle crawled backward.

Scowling and shaking his head, Grady held out his hand palm up. One of his minions removed a gun from the inside of his jacket and placed it on Grady's palm.

Noelle tried not to cry. She had to convince Grady not to kill her. She couldn't die. Beanie would be devastated. Thinking of her precious little boys growing up without their mother brought a torrent of gasping tears she couldn't contain.

Wrapping his hand around the butt of the gun, Grady slammed the firearm against her head. Crying out, Noelle fell on her side, panting from the pain reverberating beneath her skull. Pushing herself up, Noelle stared at dark drops on the floor. She touched her forehead and winced when she saw the bright red blood on her fingers. Her pulse racing, Noelle stared at Grady.

"Please don't kill me," she whispered, barely able to breathe. "Please. I'll do anything."

"Yeah, I know," Grady said, pointing the gun at her. "You will do anything to save your own sorry ass which is why you tried to set me up."

"No, Grady, I promise I didn't—"

"Shut up!" Grady crouched in front of her and pressed the gun against her forehead. "Stuck-up bitch. You think you're so much better than everybody because you got out of Handweg and went to America and got a college degree but you haven't changed."

Noelle trembled, feeling as though her heart was trying to beat its way out of her chest.

"You're still a Handweg Ho," Grady said, giving her a grim smile. "You proved that when you killed that college boy. Beat him to death with a shovel. Now, that's some Handweg shit. And after you're dead, your husband is gonna find out the truth about you. Maybe he'll write the story for *Palmchat Gazette*. Maybe the headline will be—"

"What's going on, Grady?"

Noelle jumped at the voice coming from the left. Deep and resonant with confidence and authority, the baritone was familiar, but with her mind in shambles, Noelle couldn't discern who the man was.

"What's happening here?"

The gun barrel moved from its spot between her eyes as Grady jumped up.

"Nico ..." Grady said, shock and fear in his tone.

Nico? Nicolas Lecrae? Noelle felt faint. Nicholas "Nico" Lecrae was the leader of the PC-5 in St. Killian, a direct descent of one of the original founding members of the gang. What was Nico doing here? Hesitant, Noelle glanced left as she scooted back, trying to put distance between Grady and herself.

Followed by more than a dozen PC-5 members, Nico Lecrae strode toward Grady. Tall and muscular, he was still as handsome as he was ruthless. Noelle had only had two or three encounters with Nico, fifteen years ago, but he'd been charming and nice to her.

Standing still, with the gun hanging limply at his side, Grady took a few steps back while his four goons looked worried and afraid, as though they weren't quite sure what to do.

"You need to start explaining, right now, what the hell is going on here," Nico demanded.

Noelle stared at him. Dressed in tailored slacks and a shirt made of some luxurious fabric that clung to his muscles, he was good-looking with that hint of danger that many women craved. When he caught her gaze, she saw the recognition in his green eyes.

"This bitch is a snitch," said Grady, a slight tremor beneath the bravado and disgust in his voice. "See this here?" He pointed the toe of his Italian leather loafers toward the video watch he'd destroyed. "It looked like a watch, but it was really a camera, and she was wearing it because she was trying to get evidence against me."

Arms folded across his muscular chest, Nico looked amused. "And what evidence was Dr. Bean trying to get on you?"

Noelle was surprised Nico had called her Dr. Bean. Maybe, unlike Grady, Nico accepted that she was no longer a Handweg Ho and was willing to respect her accomplishments.

"Well, you know ..." Grady glanced left and right, seemingly every-where except at Nico. "I think she's working with her husband. He works for the newspaper. I think he's trying to do an expose on me, maybe."

Watching the exchange between the two gang leaders, Noelle was torn. Did she stay still and hope Nico would allow her to leave? Or, should she get up and make a mad dash for the door Nico and his dirty dozen had entered? Every instinct told her to run. She sensed conflict between the men. Nico's distrusting scowl deepened the more Grady stammered and stuttered lame explanations. Nico was not pleased with Grady, but that didn't mean the St. Killian PC-5 leader would cut her any slack. Still, the door was far from where she sat. Glancing around the cavernous space, she realized what it was—an airplane hangar. The PC-5 had several small planes and jets at their disposal. The hangar was probably one of the gang's many legitimately purchased properties.

Nico said, "You know what, Grady? I think Dr. Bean was trying to get evidence that you were trying to force her to help you start your own pharmaceutical company."

"What?" Grady tried to sound surprised, but the fear in his voice was tangible, palpable, spreading to his four crew members who looked ready to abandon his rapidly sinking ship. "No, Nico, I don't know why you would think that man. I'm not trying to start nothing without running it by you. Nico, you know I wouldn't try no crazy shit like that."

"I think you did try some crazy shit like that," said Nico, stepping closer to Grady, invading his space. "You went behind my back, and you tried to convince Dr. Bean to supply you with prescription pain medication."

"What?" Again, Grady sounded more afraid than affronted. "Nico, you know I wouldn't—"

"You absolutely would," Nico said, glaring at Grady. "You shouldn't have, but since you did, we're going to have to have a little talk."

Grady said, "Nico, man, you can't believe that—"

"Don't say another word," Nico warned. "The sound of your voice is pissing me off."

Grady opened his mouth to protest, but two of Nico's dirty dozen shook their heads. Instantly, Grady closed his mouth and dropped his head.

Nico turned and looked down at Noelle. "Sorry about all this, Dr. Bean," he said, holding out a hand.

Noelle placed her trembling hand in his and allowed him to help her up.

After telling his dirty dozen he would return in a moment, Nico escorted Noelle to the side door of the hangar. On shaky legs, finding it hard to believe she hadn't been shot in the head, Noelle stepped outside into the bright, blazing late afternoon sunshine.

Blinking her eyes, Noelle stared up at the expansive blue sky and the white cottony clouds. The breeze slanting across her face, with its faint scent of ocean and tuberose, brought tears to her eyes. Noelle hadn't thought she would ever experience another beautiful St. Killian afternoon.

"How long has it been? Fifteen years?" Nico asked, smiling as he tilted his head. "Long damn time. A lot of changes."

Noelle nodded. "Yeah."

"The changes have been good for you," Nico said. "I'm glad you overcame and got your life on track. My grandfather and his brother fought so that a girl from Handweg could grow up and be what you've become. Really proud of you, Noelle."

"Thank you," Noelle said, somewhat touched by his sincerity and yet disturbed by the idea of a ruthless gang member admiring her.

"You should get that cut on your head taken care of," Nico said and then pointed to something behind her. "Saul will drive you back to the Purple Gecko to get your car."

Noelle glanced over her shoulder. Several luxury cars were parked in a semi-circle a few feet from the hangar. A short, thin man wearing sunglasses stood in front of a dark Bentley—Nico's car, Noelle assumed.

When she turned to thank Nico again, he'd turned from her and was walking back to the door leading into the hangar.

As Noelle walked to the Bentley, she heard a sound that sent a chill of apprehension through her.

An agonizing scream.

Chapter Thirty-One

Beanie walked into the foyer of the modest two-bedroom bungalow in the Oyster Farms neighborhood.

Closing the door behind him, Beanie tossed his keys on the side table, anxious to tell Noelle about his trip to confront Kevin Cook which hadn't turned out how he'd expected.

Things had turned out better than expected. Maybe. Hopefully.

Seeing those rusty smears on a pair of jeans that belonged to Kevin Cook had been beyond shocking. Beanie had been floored, his emotions swinging from euphoria to doubt. Everything within him wanted to shout in triumph, but he had to temper his anxiousness to celebrate.

First of all, he didn't know if the blood on the jeans was Eamon Taylor's blood. He didn't know if the jeans really belonged to Kevin Cook. For all anyone knew, the jeans could have been hidden in the bottom of the laundry basket by any one of Cook's friends or acquaintances.

Officer Damon Fields had pointed out all the things to consider after he, Sophie, and Sarah had called the St. Killian police following Sarah's bombshell reveal. Initially, the babysitter had balked at calling the police. She didn't want Kevin to get in trouble. She was afraid that

Kevin had killed Eamon but she loved him and didn't want him to be arrested. Sophie had convinced her that the cops needed to find out the truth and if Sarah had evidence to help their investigation, then she owed it to Eamon Taylor to tell the police her suspicions of Kevin and show them the bloodstained jeans.

Officer Fields hadn't been as enthusiastic as Beanie had hoped. He'd taken Sarah's statement and bagged the jeans for processing. Fields promised to follow up on the leads, and then he left after telling Beanie and Sophie to leave the investigating to the police.

Heading into the living room, Beanie paused. It was dark in the house and quiet—unnaturally so. He looked at his watch. A little after four in the afternoon. Was Noelle home? This morning, she'd told him she had to run errands, but she should be back by now.

Beanie went to the kitchen and then into the home office. Both areas were empty, and the lights were off.

"Noelle?" He called out, but not too loud just in case she and the boys were napping. "Noelle?" From the study, Beanie meandered past the powder room and then turned onto the hall leading to the bedrooms at the back of the house. He poked his head into the room the boys shared. It was dark and empty. Beanie's heart lurched. Apprehensive, he walked toward the door at the end of the hall—the master bedroom. The door was closed. He knocked softly.

"Noelle?" Beanie opened the door.

The bedroom was dark. The shades were drawn, but Beanie could make out a shape lying on the Queen-sized bed.

"Noelle?" Beanie asked, lingering by the door. "You awake?"

After a few seconds of silence, he heard, "Yeah ..."

Beanie's pulse went wild. Noelle's voice was hoarse and thick. He could tell she'd been crying. His heart broke anytime Noelle was sad or upset. All he wanted to do was make everything better.

"Why are you laying in here in the dark?" Beanie asked, trying not to jump to any dire conclusions. "You have a headache?"

"Don't turn on the light," she mumbled. "I don't want you to get upset."

"Why would I get upset if I turned on the light?"

When Noelle didn't answer, Beanie walked to the bed, crawled across the mattress and lay down behind his wife. "Babe, what's the matter?"

"I don't want to talk about it," Noelle said as she turned toward him. Clinging to him, she burst into tears and buried her face against his chest.

Worried, Beanie let her cry. When the tears subsided, Beanie rose up to reach across Noelle and turn on the bedtable lamp. "Sweetheart, what is the—"

Beanie stopped, staring at Noelle, who had moved onto her back. Fear and anger slashed through him like a machete as his eyes roamed over her face. Plum-colored bruises stained her cheeks and a nasty gash, crusted with coagulated blood, split the skin on her forehead.

"Noelle, who did this?" Beanie asked, trying to stay calm even though he felt rabid and wanted to rip something apart. "What happened to you? Who did this?"

"I messed up, Beanie," Noelle sobbed. "I was so stupid."

"What are you talking about?" Beanie asked. "What happened?"

"I'm not the woman that you think I am," she said, closing her eyes as the tears ran down her cheeks. "I don't deserve you, Beanie. I don't deserve to be your wife or the mother of—"

"Noelle, why would you say something like that?" Beanie pulled her to a sitting position. "Tell me what the hell is going on!"

Sniffing, Noelle looked down. "I was stupid to think I could be something I'm not."

"Babe, what does that mean?"

"I thought I could have a successful career and be a loving wife and mother."

"You are those things and so much more," Beanie said, confused and concerned. Noelle was usually tenacious and determined. She never gave up and always believed she could overcome any obstacles in her path, but these damn ridiculous murder charges were threatening to break her spirit.

"No, Beanie, I'm not," Noelle said, twisting from him to move off the bed. "I'm just a Handweg Ho."

Beanie shook his head, though Noelle had her back to him and couldn't see him. "You're not a Handweg Ho. You got out of Handweg.

That place is behind you. You're not about that Handweg life. You never were."

Noelle faced him, her eyes blazing with some strange emotion he couldn't identify. "I was about that Handweg life, Beanie. That's what I mean when I say I'm not the woman you think I am. I did make it out of Handweg, and I made a better life for myself but before I left ..."

"Before you left, what?"

Noelle sighed, rubbing her arms. "There are things you don't know about me, Beanie. Things you should know. Things I never wanted to tell you because I didn't want you to know the truth about me."

Beanie tensed, worried about the direction of the conversation, which he wasn't sure he wanted to have. "What is the truth about you?"

Gingerly wiping her bruised cheeks, Noelle said, "Before I left Handweg, I ... "

Waiting for Noelle to speak, Beanie fought the urge to stop her from saying anything. He feared what she was about to say, but something told him he needed to hear it.

Squaring her shoulders, Noelle said, "I used to be in the PC-5 ..."

Chapter Thirty-Two

Near the foot of the bed, perched on the edge, Noelle stared at her bare toes as she waited for Beanie's reaction.

He knew the awful truth about her now.

She could only hope he didn't hate her, but she was bracing herself for the worst—not that she would be able to withstand Beanie's wrath.

For the past few hours, Noelle had been pacing around the bedroom, staring at the bed, the dresser, the wardrobe, the night-stands, looking anywhere except at Beanie. Telling Beanie the story of her life as a fifteen-year-old PC-5 member, the life she'd escaped, Noelle hadn't wanted to see his face as she recounted her tale.

Noelle had started from the beginning when she was Noelle Chartres. Born on the wrong side of the island in Handweg Gardens, she'd lived with her mother, Natalie Chartres.

She'd moved on to her life as a tough-as-nails, take-no-prisoners juvenile delinquent with a list of misdemeanors on her long rap sheet. During that time, she'd been a defiant member of the PC-5, a legacy member through her father, Josue Chartres. Currently incarcerated in prison in St. Cera, serving a life sentence, Josue Chartres had been a violent enforcer for the PC-5.

When she was fifteen years old, Noelle had tried to explain she'd had no direction and little guidance and supervision from her mother, who had to work three jobs to afford the roach-infested four-room clapboard house they barely survived in.

The PC-5 became Noelle's family, providing her with the attention and sense of belonging she longed for, even though the love they gave her was conditional. The PC-5 required her to be a look-out and a "sticky finger," a petty thief who stole from tourists and shoplifted items the PC-5 leaders needed or wanted. She was given the street name "Nobody" because she was a sneaky thief and after she left a place where she'd hit, it would appear that "nobody" had been there.

"I always thought Nobody was an appropriate name," Noelle had said. "Back then, I felt like a nobody going nowhere and with nothing to show for my life."

The PC-5 had made her feel like somebody, she'd explained to Beanie. The gang tricked her into thinking she was tough and badass, confident and independent. Soon, the PC-5 had bigger plans for her. Her talents were wasted as a thief, according to her faction leader had claimed.

"What were these bigger plans?" Beanie had asked.

Noelle had hesitated, ashamed to tell him, but eventually, she confessed. "I started selling drugs. Mostly weed and coke to rich European tourists. I wasn't really good at it, though. After I lost a big shipment, they wanted to kill me, but they didn't."

"Why not?"

"Because of my dad," Noelle had explained. "He could have ratted on the PC-5 to stay out of jail or get a lighter sentence, but he didn't. He was loyal to the gang, and they owed him, so they spared my life. Not that it was much of a life."

Quickly, Noelle had wrapped up her sad tale of woe.

After learning about her association with the gang, Noelle's mother made the bold decision to send her to the United States to live with Remus "Remy Martin" August, her mother's brother. Remus August was a liquor distributor who'd left the Palmchat Islands when his business grew and took up residence in Washington D.C.

"And you know what happened after that," Noelle had said. "I went to college and then pharmacy school, and then I came back here to work, and you and I met and ..."

A long, sad exhale cut through the tense silence permeating the bedroom. Noelle bit her lip, trying not to cry, waiting for the backlash she knew was coming.

"Noelle, I'm glad you told me the truth about your past," said Beanie. "But, I want you to know—"

"Look, if you hate me and don't want to have anything to do with me anymore, I understand." Noelle stood and faced Beanie, who sat on the left side of the bed, closer to the headboard. "But, please—"

"How could you think that I would ever hate you?" Beanie asked, staring at her. "I love you, Noelle, and I always will. I'll never stop."

Shocked by his compassion and affection, Noelle said, "But I told you who I really am."

"I already know who you really are," Beanie said, standing. "And I don't care who you used to be or what you used to do. That doesn't matter to me. You used to be in a gang—"

"Not just any gang, Beanie," she said, confused by his lack of anger and disgust. "The PC-5. A violent, ruthless gang that's involved with drugs and—"

"You're not that person anymore," said Beanie, walking to Noelle. "You did some bad things and made decisions you regret, but that is in the past. That stuff doesn't define you, okay? You overcame your past, and that's what I love about you."

Noelle sobbed quietly as Beanie put his arms around her, holding her close.

"I hate that you didn't tell me because you thought I would judge you," Beanie said. "Who am I to throw stones at you? Have I lived a perfect life? No. I've made mistakes. Done things I regret."

"I was afraid I would lose you." Clinging to Beanie, Noelle stared at the handsome face she adored. "I was scared you wouldn't want a former PC-5 Handweg Ho to be the mother of your children."

"I don't care about what you used to be, Noelle. You have to believe me," Beanie said. "You are the only woman I want to be with, and I am so blessed to have you as my wife, and you are the best mother to our little boys."

Blinking through her tears, Noelle asked, "You really mean that?"

"Every word," said Beanie, leaning to press his lips gently against hers. "With all my heart ..."

Chapter Thirty-Three

"Mom said she is thrilled to have the boys stay overnight with her," said Noelle as she closed the bedroom door behind her. "We have the house all to ourselves. So, what do you want to do?"

Noelle ran to Beanie, who stood at the foot of the bed with his back to her and slipped her arms around him. Pressing her face against his back, she giggled softly.

Turning to her, Beanie stepped back and crossed his arms.

Her smile fading, Noelle's heart lurched. "What is it?"

"I still can't believe that you went to see Grady Palmer without me."

Beanie hadn't been upset about her PC-5 confession, but he was livid about her decision to handle the situation with Grady Palmer by herself. She'd told him after he'd demanded to know who had put the bruises on her face.

"What if you had been killed, Elle?" Beanie paced back and forth in front of the bed.

"I know I shouldn't have gone to meet him without telling you," said Noelle, knowing she couldn't tell Beanie about the gun Grady had pressed against her head. "But, I knew I would be recording the conversation with Grady, and I was afraid he would say something about my past with the PC-5 and I didn't want you to find out that way."

"You didn't want me to find out at all," Beanie reminded her.

"I'm sorry I kept it from you."

"I understand why you didn't think you could tell me," said Beanie, taking a pause from his pacing to pull her back into his embrace. "What I don't understand is ... did you think I wouldn't be able to protect you because Grady Palmer is PC-5? Did you think I would ever let anybody hurt you?"

"I know you wouldn't let anybody hurt me," Noelle said, pulling back to look at Beanie. "I was just trying to keep my past hidden. Grady had been insulting me, saying I was still a Handweg Ho and that you didn't know who I really was and I was just convinced that—"

"I would hate you," said Beanie. "Which is ridiculous."

"I know it seems irrational," Noelle admitted.

"Elle, I really do understand why you didn't tell me," Beanie said. "I just ... I want to break Grady Palmer's neck for putting his hands on you."

"Nico Lecrae probably beat you to it," Noelle said, remembering the disturbing screams coming from the airport hangar.

Beanie shook his head. "I have to thank a PC-5 gang leader for saving your life."

"Nico wasn't there to save my life," Noelle said. "He was there to give Grady hell."

"Because, as it turned out, Grady was trying to start a pill farm without Nico's permission."

"That's what I figured," said Noelle. "Grady must have a death wish. Trying to run a side hustle behind Nico's back and thinking Nico wouldn't find out?"

"Well, I guess Grady Palmer will get what he deserves," Beanie said. "I just hate that you didn't get the evidence we need to prove your innocence, but ..."

"But?" Noelle asked, noticing the astonishment on Beanie's face. "What is it?"

"Just remembering that when I came home, I had something important to tell you," Beanie said. "It's about Kevin Cook."

"Kevin Cook?" Noelle asked. "He was in the intern program. What did you want to tell me about him?"

Beanie said, "I think he may have killed Eamon Taylor."

Chapter Thirty-Four

"Before we get to what I want to discuss with you, I have some news," said Octavia Constant, taking a seat on the couch in her temporary office, the plush Queen Palm hotel suite where Noelle and Beanie had first met with her several days ago.

Sitting next to Beanie on the couch across from Octavia, Noelle grabbed Beanie's hand and braced herself. News about what? The blood on those jeans found in Kevin Cook's laundry basket? Noelle was still trying to wrap her mind around what Beanie had told her. An anonymous tip to the *Palmchat Gazette* fingering Kevin Cook as Eamon's killer and evidence that might implicate the intern in the brutal murder. Noelle wasn't sure if she should hope for the best while expecting the worse. As much as she wanted—and needed—to find Eamon's real killer, she was finding it hard to believe it was Kevin Cook

Three days had passed since Noelle had tried to get the evidence against Grady Palmer. After her plan had gone wrong, she and Beanie had spent the past two days critically discussing her encounter with Grady. Recalling her ordeal in painstaking detail, several times, Noelle had detailed everything she remembered from the meeting.

Based on Grady's responses to Noelle's attempt to trap him into telling the truth, she and Beanie didn't think Grady had Eamon killed to force Noelle to help with the pill farm. Grady seemed to think Noelle had really killed Eamon Taylor. Noelle had initially thought Grady's offer to help would be some sort of admission that he'd ordered Eamon's murder. Grady, however, had planned to taint the jury in her favor so she wouldn't be convicted.

With no evidence to help her case, she and Beanie had decided not to tell Octavia about Noelle's ordeal with the PC-5. Instead, Beanie had informed Octavia about Kevin Cook and the evidence which might point to him as the better suspect.

"Yesterday afternoon, I spoke with the police about Kevin Cook," Octavia said. "Officer Fields told me that the forensics team analyzed the denim jeans given to them by Sarah Linde which were found in the laundry basket in Kevin Cook's apartment."

"Was it Eamon Taylor's blood?" Asked Beanie, leaning forward.

Octavia shook her head. "Unfortunately, no, it wasn't."

"Whose blood was it?" Noelle asked, feeling as though the wind had been knocked from her, realizing she had been hoping against hope that the evidence would confirm Kevin Cook as Eamon Taylor's killer.

"It wasn't blood," said Octavia. "It was latex paint."

"Latex paint?" Beanie shook his head. "You're kidding."

"I wish I was," Octavia said. "Officer Fields told me that when they questioned Sarah again, she suddenly remembered that, oh yeah, Kevin and some friends had helped another friend paint a barn and he'd gotten paint on his pants."

Trying to ignore her disappointment, Noelle asked, "What about the anonymous tip sent to the *Palmchat Gazette*? Were the cops able to trace the email?"

"All they know is that the email was sent from a computer with an IP address registered to the University of St. Killian's library," Octavia said.

Noelle asked, "Can the police find out who sent the email?"

"The name on the email was Anonymous Tip," said Octavia. "The computers at the university are all public access so anyone on the island could have logged on and sent that email to the newspaper."

Rubbing her eyes, Noelle tried not to cry. Her husband's firm grip, a show of solidarity and strength, didn't seem strong enough to temper her disappointment and the feeling of hopelessness threatening to drown her.

"Once again, we need to focus on showing the police that Noelle could not have killed Eamon Taylor," said Octavia. "I realize that's easier said than done especially since the evidence against Noelle makes her look beyond guilty."

"Did you find out if Eamon Taylor had any enemies?" Beanie asked.

"My cousin Icarus did speak with a few of Eamon Taylor's relatives and some of his friends from Handweg Gardens, where he grew up," said Octavia, "and no one had a bad word to say about him. His family is devastated and can't imagine why anyone would want to hurt him. His friends can't believe he was murdered because he was never in any trouble. Even though he grew up in a rough neighborhood, he didn't succumb to the normal pressures that young men from disenfranchised areas fall prey to. He didn't get into drugs, never accidentally got a girl pregnant, and didn't get involved in gang life."

Noelle took in a quick breath, ashamed of how she'd given in to the dangerous seduction of the PC-5, but when Beanie squeezed her hand, she remembered the past was behind her. There was no reason to condemn herself for her former mistakes.

"However, Icarus found out that Eamon owed money to the PC-5," said Octavia. "Apparently, he borrowed money from them to pay his university tuition. He was having problems paying the gang back. The police found threatening text messages on his cell phone about some debt he needed to pay. We have to consider that maybe the PC-5 killed him. I've got Icarus looking into that theory."

Noelle said, "I don't think the PC-5 killed Eamon."

"How can you be so sure that they didn't?" Octavia asked. "Eamon owed them money. They threatened him. They may have killed him because he didn't pay them back."

Shaking her head, Noelle said, "Well, I know Grady Palmer didn't kill him."

"Who is Grady Palmer?" Octavia asked.

"Son of a bitch who tried to get Noelle hemmed up in a pill farm scam," said Beanie.

"A pill farm scam?" Octavia exhaled. "Okay, start at the beginning, please, and don't leave anything out."

After a long sigh, Noelle told Octavia everything about her involvement with Grady Palmer, starting from the very beginning—fifteen years ago—and ending with those horrible moments in the PC-5 airplane hangar, when Noelle had been certain she would be shot to death.

Following a stern rebuke of Noelle's dangerous plan, Octavia said, "Well, just because Grady Palmer didn't kill Eamon doesn't mean Nico Lecrae didn't put a hit out on him. I want Icarus to dig deeper. We need a better suspect. The police still believe Noelle was the only person who had beef with Eamon Taylor."

"Because she confronted Eamon about those bogus harassment claims?" Beanie asked.

"I never sexually harassed Eamon," said Noelle. "I would never do that."

"But Eamon Taylor was a good-looking guy," said Octavia, a hint of devil's advocate in her tone. "You never once wondered what it would be like if the two of you—"

"Never," said Noelle, her denial adamant. "I have a husband I love and adore. I'm not interested in any other man. I don't care how good-looking he is."

"Well, the evidence seems to suggest that you were interested in Eamon Taylor." Octavia stood and went to the desk in the far right corner of the living area. After removing a file from her briefcase, she returned to the couch. "The police believe they have Noelle's motive for the murder, which is that she killed Eamon because she was afraid he would sue her and she'd be fired."

"Before he was killed, Eamon told me, when I confronted him, that he had proof that I had harassed him," said Noelle. "He never showed it to me, though."

"I'm glad you brought that up," Octavia said. "I have the so-called proof in this file. The police spoke to an attorney named George Gaston."

"I know about him," Noelle said. "He sent me the letter saying that he wanted to mediate a settlement concerning the harassment claims."

"Do I have that letter?" Octavia asked. "If not, I need it. But, as I was saying, the police spoke to Attorney Gaston, who told them that Eamon provided him with copies of emails you supposedly sent to him. When Attorney Gaston saw the emails, he decided to take the case, thinking it would be a slam dunk."

Noelle shook her head. "I never sent Eamon Taylor any emails. I mean, I did, but they were always related to the internship program. And I never sent any emails just to him specifically. The emails were sent to all the interns in a group email."

"That admission only helps to convince the police that you sent the emails because you did have Eamon's email address," said Octavia.

"I'm not the only one who had his damn address," Noelle said, her temper flaring but then Beanie's firm pressure calmed her down a bit.

"What do the emails say?" Beanie asked.

"The messages are rather lewd," said Octavia, opening the file. "What concerns me, even more, is that the first email Eamon Taylor received was sent from a computer located at your address."

"Our address?" Noelle was confused.

"That's impossible."

"The police traced the IP address to a computer located at your home address," Octavia maintained. "So how did that happen? Could anyone besides the two of you have had access to your home computer?"

Beanie shook his head. "No. We only have one computer. It's in the home office and Elle, and I are the only ones who use it."

"That's what I was afraid of," said Octavia.

"How many emails are there?" Beanie asked.

"Four or five, I think," said Octavia, shuffling through the contents of the file. "Only one email came from your computer. The other emails came from an unknown IP address which was probably a burner with internet and data capabilities."

"And my name is on these emails?" Noelle asked.

"The emails are signed 'Dr. Bean'," said Octavia. "The email addresses aren't any of your official addresses, but the police think you created fake email addresses and used a burner to cover your tracks."

"This is crazy," Noelle said. "How am I supposed to prove I didn't send those emails?"

"You let me worry about that," said Octavia.

"Can I have copies of the emails?" Beanie asked, and Octavia agreed to make copies on her portable copier.

"One more thing," she said, flipping through more papers in the file. "I found out that the police talked to the residents at the apartment complex where Eamon Taylor lived. The building has eight apartments. The police were asking if anyone had seen anything suspicious when Eamon was killed. No one claimed to have seen anything. However, when I looked at the reports, I noticed that the officer who did the interviews only spoke to six of the eight residents. Two of the residents were not home at the time. Mr. Stanley Reese in apartment three and Ted Chen in apartment seven. However, there is no report of the officer going back to talk to those two residents, probably because of the strong evidence against Noelle."

"You need to talk to those two residents," said Noelle, daring to hope. "Maybe one of them saw something or someone."

"Maybe they saw the person who killed Eamon Taylor," said Beanie.

Octavia nodded. "Icarus had to fly to St. Cera on business, but he's coming back tomorrow, and I'm going to have him talk to the residents the officer didn't interview."

Chapter Thirty-Five

"Did you forget we need to pick up the boys from my mom's?" asked Noelle when Beanie turned the SUV right instead of left onto the main boulevard in front of the Queen Palm hotel.

"We're not going to pick up the boys right now," said Beanie, passing a slower car as he sped down the road, heading farther away from the streets which led to Handweg Gardens.

"Why not?" Noelle asked, concerned about her husband's clenched jaw. "Where are we going?"

"We're going to talk to those residents the police didn't interview," said Beanie, clutching the steering wheel. "The guy in apartment three and the guy in apartment seven."

"We are?" Noelle took a quick breath.

"You have Eamon Taylor's address?"

"I think I have it in my contacts on my phone," Noelle said. "I had to send the interns dinner invitations and some other paperwork."

"You find it, and we'll head over there."

"You think we should?" Noelle asked, uncertain about Beanie's plan. "Octavia's cousin—"

"We don't need to wait for her cousin," Beanie said. "We need to find out right now if those two men know anything."

Warming to the idea, Noelle asked, "You think they'll talk to us?"

"I'm a journalist, babe," Beanie said, giving her a quick glance and comforting smile. "I know how to ask the right questions. If either of those two guys know anything, I'm going to get them to tell us."

Twenty minutes later, Beanie was handing a business card to the bleary-eyed old Asian man who finally opened the door to apartment seven after they'd knocked about a hundred damn times. Discouraged by the absence of the resident in apartment three, Noelle had grown frustrated by her husband's dogged persistence. The manager of the Sea Glass Villages, a twentyish Barbie doll with a disposition as sunny as her gleaming blonde hair, was sorry to tell them that Stanley Reese, who resided in number three, hadn't been home since he'd gotten a job on an oil rig off the coast of Venezuela. Ted Chen, in apartment seven, was probably home, though.

After the tenth knock, Noelle told Beanie they should forget about trying to talk to Ted Chen. The man either wasn't home or didn't want to be bothered. Their trip to the Sea Glass Village, a cluster of small Caribbean-Dutch apartments surrounded by a courtyard, had seemed like a good idea twenty minutes ago but Noelle was no longer in the mood to play Nancy Drew. She just wanted to pick up the boys from her mom's place, go home, and maybe try to relax.

She'd been about to insist that they leave when the door opened.

"I'm Roland Bean from the *Palmchat Gazette*," said Beanie. "I'm working on a story for the newspaper and wondered if I could ask you a few questions."

The Asian man squinted and scowled as he stared at Beanie's card. "I don't know nothing."

"Maybe you know more than you think," said Beanie. "I want to ask about your neighbor Eamon Taylor. He lived in the studio apartment."

"Across the way," said the old man, tilting his head in the direction across the small courtyard to the door with an "8" mounted above the peephole. "What do you want to know about him?"

"Did you hear about what happened to him?" Beanie asked.

Noelle took a step back, deciding to let Beanie do his thing, which he was better at than she'd realized. His style was interesting and impressive, conversational and yet probing. With his winning smile and compassionate demeanor, he steadily put Ted Chen at ease. Initially, the older man had been tense and suspicious, but now his shoulders and his stern expression were relaxed.

Ted Chen shook his head. "It's a shame. Who would do such a horrible thing? He wasn't a bad guy."

"So, you knew Eamon?"

"Oh, yeah," said Ted Chen, nodding. "He was a good neighbor. Nice guy. Didn't make a lot of noise or have a bunch of people over or have a lot of wild parties."

"The day Eamon was killed," Beanie said, "were you at home that day?"

"What day was that?"

Beanie told him, and then said, "The police think he was killed around noon."

Ted Chen said, "I was home, but I didn't hear nothing."

"Are you sure?" Noelle couldn't stop herself from asking. "You didn't see anything unusual?"

"Did you see anyone?" Beanie asked. "Did you notice if he had a visitor around that time?"

"No, I didn't," said Ted Chen, frowning. "I didn't see nothing then but ..."

"But what?" Beanie asked.

Noelle took a deep breath and cautioned herself not to expect a smoking gun revelation.

"I did see something strange the next day," Ted Chen said. "It was that night, actually."

"What did you see that was strange?" Beanie asked.

"I saw someone come out of Eamon's apartment," Ted Chen said. "At the time, I didn't know what had happened to him. It was a little after midnight. It wasn't Eamon, though."

"Do you know who it was?" Beanie asked. "Did you recognize the person?"

"No, it was too dark," Ted Chen said. "But, I could tell it was a guy. He came out of Eamon's place carrying two suitcases. I was out with my dog. He has a weak bladder. Wakes me up all times of the night because he has to go. So, I was coming back to my apartment when I saw the guy leaving Eamon's apartment with the suitcases. I thought maybe it was a friend or a relative. The person hurried out to the back parking lot and, well sometimes I don't mind my own business, so I kind of followed, but I stayed out of sight."

"And then what?" Beanie prompted.

"The man put the suitcases in the back seat and then drove off."

"Did you see what kind of car it was?" Beanie asked.

"A red car," said Ted Chen. "Looked like a little four-door sedan."

Moments later, as they drove away from the Sea Glass Village apartments, Noelle asked,"What do you think about what Ted Chen told us?"

Beanie said, "I think he saw Eamon Taylor's killer."

"How can we know that for sure?" Noelle bit her bottom lip. As soon as Ted Chen told them about the mystery guy leaving Eamon's place with two suitcases, Noelle had jumped to the same conclusion. She didn't want to the get her hopes up and thought it might be best to make sure their theory held up under scrutiny.

"What else are we supposed to think, Elle?" Beanie asked. "A guy comes out of Eamon's apartment after midnight carrying two suitcases. And then he takes those suitcases and puts them into a red car. A red four-door sedan like your red four-door sedan that was stolen from you before Eamon was killed. The only thing I can think is that Ted Chen saw Eamon's killer carrying suitcases which contained Eamon's hacked up dead body."

"But we don't know that it was my red car," Noelle said. "Ted Chen didn't get a license plate number."

"Octavia said we need to find another suspect."

"She said to find a better suspect," Noelle clarified. "A guy that Ted Chen didn't get a good look at who took suitcases from Eamon's apartment is not exactly a better suspect. We don't have a name for this mystery guy. We don't have a description."

"True, but still," said Beanie, "we need to tell the police there's more information about Eamon's murder that they need to consider. We need to tell the cops to talk to Ted Chen."

Nodding, Noelle said, "He did say he was willing to tell the police what he told us."

"That's what has to happen," Beanie said. "The information can't come from us. It has to come from Ted Chen."

"We need to tell Octavia, too," said Noelle.

"Give her a call," said Beanie, steering the SUV around a curve in the road. "Tell her to meet us at the police station."

Chapter Thirty-Six

"Did Octavia call with any news about whether or not the cops went to talk to Ted Chen?" Beanie asked.

"No, not yet," said Noelle, walking across the kitchen to the sink. "And what are you doing here? Did you tell me you were coming home for lunch today?"

A few days had passed since she and Beanie had talked to Ted Chen. Their trip to the police department hadn't inspired much confidence in the department's willingness to investigate the mysterious guy Chen had seen leaving Eamon's apartment. Officer Fields didn't think Chen's information warranted further investigation, but Octavia convinced him that he should interview Eamon's neighbor and take his statement. As Octavia pointed out, Ted Chen would have been—and in fact, should have been—interviewed if he'd been home when the original officer had spoken to the other residents at the complex.

"I'm actually not here for lunch," said Beanie, tossing a thick file folder on the table in the breakfast nook before taking a seat.

At the refrigerator, Noelle paused, not sure if she should make Beanie a sandwich with last night's roasted goat. Normally, her husband didn't come home for lunch because, normally, Noelle wouldn't be home at one o'clock in the afternoon. Normally, at this time, she would be beyond busy filling prescriptions and doing patient consultations at the Palmchat Pharmacy. For the time being, Noelle had a new normal—being a stay-at-home mom, which she loved and was starting to get used to. She'd always valued her career and relished her role as an accomplished working mom, but the time she'd been able to spend with Ethan and Evan had been pure joy, and she savored each moment.

But then she would remember that her "new normal" was the unintended result of the dire circumstances threatening to destroy her life. Nothing had been normal since she'd been accused of sexually harassing and then subsequently murdering Eamon Taylor. And if she was convicted of a crime she hadn't committed, then nothing would be normal ever again.

Closing the fridge, Noelle faced Beanie. "Why are you here? Stopped by for a little afternoon delight, Mr. Bean?"

"Oh, babe, I wish," said Beanie, smiling at her. "But, I may have something better than that."

"Better than sex?" she teased, trying to manage the slight flare of disappointment. The new normal had also wrecked havoc on their sex life. How could she think about making love when she was facing a murder charge? Still, she missed the intense intimacy with her husband and wondered if a quickie might get her mind off her problems, if only for a moment or two. Or three.

"Come here," Beanie said, and when she joined him at the table, he opened the file and began spreading papers across the polished wood surface.

"What's all this?" Noelle asked.

"Remember the emails I got from Octavia?" Beanie asked. "The ones that you supposedly sent Eamon Taylor?"

Noelle nodded. "Yeah, but I didn't want to read them."

"Neither did I," Beanie admitted. "But, I did."

"Were they awful?"

"Worse than awful," said Beanie. "But the point is, I think I can prove you didn't send them. That you couldn't have sent them."

Noelle's pulse jumped. "Are you serious? How?"

"I started looking at when the emails were sent," Beanie started, moving the papers around until he found the copy of the email he wanted. "The emails were sent from the account *doctor sexy milf at St. Killian univ dot com.*"

Rolling her eyes, Noelle said, "Doctor sexy MILF? As if I would ever refer to myself that way."

"Well, it's true," said Beanie. "You are a MILF."

"And you're a DILF," she said, stealing a quick kiss. "Now, tell me how you can prove I didn't send those ridiculous emails."

"The doctor sexy MILF account was initially created on at 9:49 p.m. on this date," said Beanie, pointing at the paper which showed when the account had been created. "Do you know where you were at 9:9 p.m. on that day?"

"Beanie, I can't think, okay," Noelle said, her anxiousness increasing. "Just tell me."

"You were with me," Beanie said. "At Dizzy Jenny's."

"Oh my God," said Noelle, remembering. "Date night."

"We weren't at home when this account was created on the computer in our home office," said Beanie. "How could you be at Dizzy Jenny's with me—and our waiters and servers can tell the cops they saw us there—and at home in the office creating a fake account to send dirty emails to Eamon Taylor?"

"I couldn't have been at Dizzy Jenny's and creating the fake account," said Noelle, allowing hope to rise. "But, that means someone else was creating the fake account on our computer while we were having dinner."

His expression grim, Beanie said, "That's right. So, the question is, who was at our house that night while we were at Dizzy Jenny's?"

Realization hit Noelle like a sucker punch. "Sarah? Oh, Beanie, no! Sarah couldn't have created that fake account? Why would she do something like that?"

"Why would she show the cops a pair of jeans that turned out to be stained with paint instead of blood?" Beanie asked. "Why would she say she thought Kevin Cook might have killed Eamon?"

"You think Sarah is trying to shift suspicion to Kevin and away from herself?" Noelle shook her head. "Do you think Sarah killed Eamon and is trying to frame me?"

"Sarah weighs eighty pounds soaking wet if that much," said Beanie, gathering the email copies he'd spread across the table. "I don't think she's strong enough to have beat Eamon with a shovel. But from the conversation Sophie and I had with her, I think she's easily led—by Kevin."

"Why do you think that?"

"It was clear to Sophie and me that Sarah is more in love with Kevin than he is with her," Beanie said. "Even though she told us about the jeans and Kevin's animosity toward Eamon, I could tell she didn't want to. She was upset and regretful. She kept telling the cops that she didn't want to get Kevin in trouble."

"Then why would she tell the cops that she suspected Kevin?"

"Sophie says that even people with Stockholm's Syndrome will try to escape their captors at least once," Beanie said. "Telling the cops her suspicions might have been her attempt to break free of Kevin's control. Sophie and I still don't know who sent us the anonymous tip about Kevin Cook, but we both suspect Sarah. I think that Sarah knows Kevin killed Eamon, but he's instructed her to stay quiet."

"You think Kevin told Sarah to create that doctor sexy MILF account?"

"Who else could have done it?" Beanie asked. "Sarah comes to our house to babysit. She's got unrestricted access to the computer. We've even told her she could use it if she forgets her laptop. Kevin probably knew that. So, in his plan to frame you for Eamon's murder, Kevin makes Sarah create the fake email account at our house while she's babysitting."

Shaking her head, Noelle stood and walked to the sink. Staring through the window into the backyard, she watched the remnants of her neglected rose bushes sway in the gentle afternoon ocean breeze.

Trying to process what Beanie had told her, she found it difficult to believe Sarah would participate in Kevin's scheme to frame her for Eamon Taylor's murder. According to Beanie, Sarah was weak and easily manipulated, guided by Kevin Cook's control and command. Noelle knew a different Sarah, a smart, caring, and friendly young woman, dedicated to her studies and the pursuit of her passions, which was to work in research for a Big Pharma firm.

"Elle, I want you to call Sarah?"

Noelle faced Beanie. "Why? You want me to ask her if she helped her boyfriend set me up for murder?"

"Look, I know you don't want to believe that Sarah could be involved," said Beanie. "But, you have to put your feelings aside for the sake of your freedom. Your life is at stake which means my life is at stake, and so are our boys' lives. None of us will be able to survive you going to jail for something you didn't do."

"I know that," said Noelle returning to the table.

Grabbing her hand, Beanie gave it the supportive squeeze that always comforted her. "Elle, if Kevin Cook killed Eamon—and I believe he did—then we have to prove it. Now, I also believe Kevin got Sarah to help him. I think she told me, Sophie and the cops her suspicions of Kevin because she had an attack of conscience and felt guilty about her part in his crimes."

Noelle nodded. "Maybe you're right."

"I think Sarah is our best opportunity to get proof against Kevin," said Beanie. "We have to convince her to flip on him."

"You think we can?"

"I think we have to," said Beanie. "But, as Sophie would say, we have to be sly and subtle about it. We can't scare Sarah off. We can't make her suspicious."

"So what do I say when I call?" Noelle asked.

Beanie said, "Just ask Sarah if she remembers using our computer that night?"

"What if she asks me why I'm asking?" Noelle asked. "She probably will."

"Tell her that you found some photos that you don't recognize and you wonder if she used the computer to email those photos to someone," Beanie said.

"And what if she says that she did use the computer?" Noelle asked.

"Then you ask her why," said Beanie. "See what she says. The key is not to accuse her of anything. We just want to confirm that she used the computer that night.

Noelle nodded, praying she wouldn't screw anything up.

"Another thing," said Beanie. "We want to get her on tape. So, when you call, put the phone on speaker, and I'll use my phone to record the conversation."

Despite the nervous tension coursing through her, Noelle managed to call Sarah. After the obligatory small talk about school and the boys, she got on with the business of asking Sarah about the computer.

"I didn't use the computer that night," said Sarah. "But maybe Kevin did."

"Kevin?" Noelle glanced at Beanie. "How would Kevin have used the computer? Was he there with you that night?"

Silence.

Noelle stared at Beanie who signaled her to keep talking. "Sarah ...?"

"Yeah, I'm here," said Sarah, her voice small and hollow. "I just, um ... I know I'm not supposed to have anyone over while I'm taking care of the boys and I never do, but that night, I'd forgotten a book I needed for a paper I had due the next day, and I asked Kevin to bring the book to me at your place. I'm sorry."

"No, it's okay, I understand." Noelle looked at Beanie, and when he nodded, she said, "So, you think maybe Kevin used the computer?"

"Maybe," said Sarah, her tone hesitant and noncommittal. Noelle wondered if the young woman was regretting her confession.

"Okay, well, I'll speak with Kevin."

Sarah said, "You can't."

Noelle's gaze shot to Beanie. He shared her look of confused suspicion. "Why can't I talk to Kevin?"

"If you want to talk to him in person, I mean," Sarah said. "He's still in the USVI at a seminar."

"Do you know when he's supposed to return to St. Killian?" Noelle asked.

"Maybe next week," said Sarah.

Noelle thanked Sarah for talking to her and ended the call. "So what do you think?"

Beanie said, "I think we need to call Octavia and set up a time to meet with her so she can listen to this audio. We have proof that Kevin Cook was in our house, and had access to our computer, the night that doctor sexy MILF email account was created."

Chapter Thirty-Seven

"What are the cops doing here?" Beanie whispered to Octavia as the lawyer closed the door to her opulent hotel suite.

When Beanie had called earlier to talk to Octavia about their theory that Kevin Cook had created the fake email account, he'd been surprised to learn Octavia had just been about to call them. The police had shown up unexpected and unannounced, requesting that she summon the Beans to her suite—immediately.

Standing in the foyer of the suite, Noelle tried not to panic as she stared across the living room at Detective Philippi Janvier and Officer Fields. The policemen stood close to each other, whispering intently. About what, Noelle had no clue. She couldn't help but jump to the worst conclusion—they had more damaging evidence against her.

Evidence that made her appear to look even more guilty even though she wasn't.

"They have some news about Eamon Taylor's neighbor, Ted Chen," said Octavia, her expression grave.

"What kind of news?" Beanie asked.

Noelle's heart raced. Once again, as she had so many times recently, she struggled not to think the worse, but the stern faces and rigid posture of the officers filled her with apprehension.

"Janvier and Fields wouldn't tell me," said Octavia, clearly peeved at being kept in the dark. "They wanted to wait until you arrived."

"You think Ted Chen recanted his story?" Beanie asked.

Feeling her knees weaken, Noelle fought the panic rising within her. Why would Ted Chen tell the police a different story than what he'd told her and Beanie? The information Ted Chen had shared was crucial. The police needed to know about the mysterious man who'd exited Eamon's apartment with two suitcases he'd put into the trunk of a red four-door sedan.

"I have no idea," said Octavia. "I hope not, but there's no use speculating. Let's find out why they're here."

Noelle followed Beanie and Octavia into the living area. After curt greetings, everyone took seats on the couches, and Detective Janvier said, "Thank you for agreeing to meet us. I won't belabor the point. A few days ago, you informed my colleague Officer Fields that you had spoken to a gentleman named Ted Chen. Mr. Chen, according to you, gave you information regarding the murder of Eamon Taylor."

"That's correct," said Octavia.

"Yesterday, Officer Fields attempted to determine the veracity of your claims," said Janvier.

"I went out to the Sea Glass Village apartments to talk to Ted Chen," said Officer Fields. "Unfortunately, I was unable to do so."

"Maybe he wasn't home," said Beanie. "Did you try calling him?"

"You have to talk to him," Noelle said, a sense of desperation creeping within her even though Beanie's grip was strong and supportive. "He has information that you need to know."

"I would very much like to hear what Ted Chen has to say," said Janvier. "However, it is impossible."

"Why is it impossible?" asked Octavia. "If it's a matter of locating Ted Chen, I have resources—"

"We don't need to locate Chen," said Janvier. "We know exactly where he is."

"Then I don't understand," said Noelle, glaring at the grim, unreadable faces of the lawmen. "Why can't you talk to him if you know where he is?"

Detective Janvier said, "Because Ted Chen is unable to speak with us."

Officer Fields said, "He's dead …"

Chapter Thirty-Eight

Ted Chen was dead.

Her mind both numb and swirling with questions, Noelle sat paralyzed on the couch in Octavia's hotel suite. Detective Janvier and Officer Fields had left an hour ago, but their chilling words lingered. Eamon's neighbor had suffered a gruesome fate.

Ted Chen had been savagely beaten with a box fan and then strangled to death with the extension cord connected to the portable cooling device.

Detective Janvier had admitted they had no leads, so far. No one had seen or heard anything. The crime scene had been processed, evidence collected, and the investigation was ongoing. There had been no forced entry. Janvier surmised that Chen either knew his killer or had opened the door for the grisly attacker who'd ended his life.

"The good thing is," said Octavia, glancing at Noelle, "that Janvier knows you had nothing to do with the murder of Ted Chen. There is no evidence that connects you to the killing."

"The bad thing is that Ted Chen was killed because someone found out he was going to tell the cops about the guy he saw leaving Eamon's apartment with the suitcases," said Beanie, jumping up to pace around the couches. "It is not a coincidence that Chen was killed before he could give the police crucial information that could have changed the course of their investigation—away from Noelle and toward the mystery guy."

"There's no way to know that Chen's statement would have compelled Janvier to consider another suspect," said Octavia. "What he told you was interesting, but he didn't get a clear look at the guy with the suitcases, and he didn't get any plates on the red car."

"But whoever killed him didn't know that," said Beanie. "Whoever killed Chen must have thought that maybe he could make a positive ID and maybe he had gotten the license plate of the red car."

"How would someone have known that Ted Chen was going to talk to the police?" Octavia said.

"Maybe he told someone," Beanie said, rubbing his jaw.

"You think Ted Chen spoke to Eamon's killer without knowing he was talking to the killer?" Octavia asked.

"I don't know," said Beanie, shaking his head. "All I know is that a man is dead because he was willing to help Noelle get out of this mess she doesn't deserve to be in. We finally were catching a damn break, and now it's like we're back where we started."

Dropping her head, Noelle wiped a tear before it fell. The raw fear in Beanie's voice was a horrible reminder of how her situation was affecting him.

After a low exhale, Octavia said, "I know the circumstances seem overwhelming, and I don't want to give you a trite motivational speech, but there is a light at the end of the tunnel."

Beanie scoffed. "Yeah, that light is the train speeding right at you."

Noelle wiped another tear, worried by the trace of hopelessness in Beanie's tone. If her husband fell apart, she didn't know how she would make it, but she would have to—somehow, someway. She had to keep it together and make sure she didn't go down for something she hadn't done.

"Listen, we will prove that Noelle didn't kill Eamon Taylor," said Octavia. "Noelle wasn't at home when the doctor sexy MILF email account was created. That's the first crack in the police's theory that Noelle's motive for murder was her fear of Eamon suing her for sexual harassment. If I can prove that Noelle didn't have a motive for killing Eamon, then their case will be severely weakened."

Beanie nodded. "They need means, opportunity, and motive. But good luck convincing Janvier that Kevin Cook created the fake account."

Noelle agreed. They'd been able to share that theory with the evasive, doubtful detective but he wasn't as receptive to the possibility as Noelle would have liked.

"Well, he did promise to talk to Kevin Cook about that when Cook returns to St. Killian," reminded Octavia.

If Kevin Cook returns, thought Noelle, and then immediately chided herself for being negative. Still, the thought lingered and gave her a strange, ominous feeling.

"Another thing I'm working on is tracing the burner that was used to send the emails after the fake account was created," said Octavia.

"Burners can't be traced," said Beanie.

"True, but the emails were traced to a specific phone number," agreed Octavia. "That phone number is for a burner which contains a GPS chip."

"So, you can track the GPS chip," said Beanie.

Octavia nodded. "I have someone going through the GPS data."

Beanie said, "The GPS data should show where the phone was—geographically—when those MILF emails were sent, right?"

"Hopefully," said Octavia. "If we know where the phone was located when the emails were sent, then we can prove Noelle wasn't at that location at the time."

"Unless the person who sent the emails was standing right next to me while they were being sent," said Noelle.

"What do you mean?" asked Beanie, returning to the couch.

"I've always suspected that Eamon Taylor was trying to scam me," said Noelle.

Octavia nodded. "You could be right about that. Eamon might have sent the emails to himself to extort money from you so he could pay off the PC-5."

"But before Eamon could collect any payment from me," said Noelle. "Someone killed him ..."

"Possibly the PC-5," said Octavia. "I haven't given up on that theory even though Icarus hasn't been able to confirm or deny that the gang put out a hit on Eamon for non-payment."

"Maybe we should give up on that theory," said Noelle. "If Nico Lecrae gave the order to kill Eamon then no one in Handweg is going to snitch."

Octavia said, "Well, there is potentially another possibility ..."

"What?" Beanie asked.

"The police aren't making much of it," said Octavia, "but they found some love letters in Eamon's apartment although Officer Fields showed me one of the letters and there was no love in it."

"Who wrote the letters?" Noelle asked.

"The police aren't sure," Octavia said. "But, they had a stalker-type vibe. Whoever wrote the letters seemed to have been in some sort of relationship with Eamon. This person was very upset because Eamon wasn't interested in the relationship."

"So, Eamon had a stalker?" Beanie asked.

"Could the stalker have killed him?" Noelle wondered.

"I'm not sure if the person who wrote the letters was stalking Eamon," Octavia said. "He never filed any police reports claiming that he was being stalked, but the letter I read was disturbing and could be seen as threatening."

Leaning forward, Beanie asked, "What was disturbing about the letter?"

Octavia said, "Whoever wrote the letter told Eamon that if he broke their heart, they would rip out his..."

Chapter Thirty-Nine

"You know what I think?" Beanie asked as he steered the SUV into the traffic heading left on the boulevard in front of the Queen Palm hotel.

"That some spurned lover turned stalker killed Eamon?" Noelle guessed.

Beanie shook his head. "I don't think some lovesick girl beat him in the head with a shovel because he stopped paying attention to her."

"Even though she promised to rip his heart out?"

"Some girl with a crush being melodramatic didn't kill him," Beanie said. "I was thinking about what happened to Ted Chen. Whoever killed him must have seen us talking to him which means whoever is setting you up is probably watching you."

Alarmed, she asked, "You think so?"

"They're setting you up, so they have to make sure their frame job is working," said Beanie, taking the exit to the coastal highway that ringed the island. "They can't have you figuring out the truth, you know. If they see you getting too close to the truth, they have to stop you."

"So Ted Chen's death is my fault," said Noelle, rubbing her eyes, her stomach churning from grief and guilt.

"No, babe, none of this is your fault, okay?" Beanie took one hand off the wheel to grab her hand. "Ted Chen is dead because whoever is trying to frame you is a psychopath. We gotta be careful, and we gotta start being hyper-aware of our surroundings. Anything that seems suspicious, we gotta check it out. Right now, I'm checking the cars behind us."

Heart in her throat, Noelle sat up and twisted in the seat, staring through the back window. "You think we're being followed?"

"I don't know," said Beanie. "But we have to make sure that we're not. That's why I'm taking the long way home."

Noelle shook her head and leaned back against the headrest. "This is a nightmare."

"Yeah," Beanie agreed. "But we're going to wake up soon."

Thirty minutes later, standing shirtless in the middle of their bedroom and staring at his phone, Beanie frowned.

"What is it?" Noelle sat up in bed and reached for the robe at the foot of the bed. Covering the skimpy lingerie she'd stripped down to, she stared at Beanie, worried by his apprehensive expression.

"So much for our afternoon delight," he mumbled.

Instead of picking up the boys from her mom, she and Beanie had decided the trauma of the morning warranted a few hours of selfishness. Despite her raging emotions, Noelle relished the idea of a sweaty sex session to take her mind away from her problems. Since her arrest, she and Beanie had neglected their marital duties, forgoing lovemaking in favor of legal strategy.

"What's the matter?"

"It's not anything bad," said Beanie. "The text was from Sophie. She got another anonymous tip about Kevin Cook being Eamon's killer. Only this time, she emailed the tipster back, asking to meet, and the tipster agreed. She wants to know if I want to go with her to talk to the tipster."

Noelle scrambled off the bed and hurried to Beanie. "You have to go. You have to find out why this tipster thinks Kevin killed Eamon."

Beanie sighed. "I don't want to leave you here alone. I'll take you to your mom's."

"I have a better idea," Noelle said. "Take me with you to meet the tipster."

Chapter Forty

"This is where the anonymous tipster wanted to meet?" Beanie asked Sophie as they exited the SUV.

Shocked and skeptical, Noelle surveyed her surroundings as she closed the passenger door. The area was all too familiar, a place Noelle had visited often and where she'd made many friends.

The University of St. Killian.

"I was a bit suspicious, too," said Sophie as they walked across the visitor parking lot to a wide sidewalk which traversed throughout the plantation-style buildings of the campus. "But it's a public place, so that's good."

"You have any idea who this tipster might be?" asked Noelle, falling into step with Sophie, who strode purposely between Noelle and Beanie.

A balmy breeze blew Sophie's springy curls as she shook her head. "Part of me thinks it's a student but who knows?"

"It's got to be someone who knows Kevin Cook," said Beanie, leading the way across the palm-lined quad.

"Where exactly are we supposed to meet the tipster?" Noelle asked.

Sophie checked her phone. "Um ... Lecture Hall 7a in the Collister Building. You know where that is?"

Noelle nodded. "It's where I present most of my lectures."

"Interesting," said Sophie. "Well, lead the way."

In the empty lecture hall, Noelle shivered. When was the last time she'd been in the Collister Building? The contentious confrontation of Helen Farber sprang to mind. A lifetime ago it seemed—before she'd been accused of murder. As she, Beanie and Sophie walked down the wide, flat steps to the first row of seating, Noelle wondered if her life would forever be defined by the horrible demarcation of before the murder charges and after the murder charges.

"Okay, we're here," said Beanie, turning to stare up toward the doors they'd entered. "Where's this anonymous tipster?"

As she drifted toward the lectern she'd stood behind so many time, Noelle heard a door open and turned.

Stunned, she stared at the three people heading down the stairs toward them. Familiar faces she knew well. Students who'd participated in the Palmchat Pharmacy internship program she'd recently coordinated: Jimmy Quible, Matt Delany, and Tina Chen-Soo. The interns stared back at her, confusion playing across their bewildered expressions as their gazes roamed from Noelle to Beanie to Sophie.

As they converged in the area between the first row and the presentation stage, Noelle watched their shock turn to suspicion as the trio cast furtive looks between each other.

Arms crossed, Sophie introduced herself and then asked, "Which one of you is the tipster?"

The was a tense moment of hesitation as Tina, Jimmy, and Matt fidgeted, squirmed, and glanced everywhere except at Noelle.

"Do I need to repeat the question?" Sophie asked.

The trio appeared unsure and reluctant. There were more nervous glances among them before Matt cleared his throat. "Um ... Dr. Bean, why are you here?"

"I've only met you guys once," Beanie said, casual and affable. "But I'm sure you remember that I'm Dr. Bean's husband, Roland. I work with Sophie Carter at the *Palmchat Gazette*."

"Beanie and I are helping a colleague with the Eamon Taylor

murder story," Sophie said. "So that's why Beanie is here, and Dr. Bean just tagged along. Now, the tipster is ...?"

Tina, Matt, and Jimmy still looked skeptical, but after a shrug, Tina said, "We are ... all three of us. Me, Matt and Jimmy sent the anonymous tip about Kevin Cook killing Eamon Taylor."

Chapter Forty-One

After coaxing the interns to take a seat in the front row, Sophie and Beanie stood in front of them, authoritative and confident as they began the questioning.

Noelle decided to stand near the lectern, content to allow Sophie and Beanie to do what they did best without any interruption from her. The last thing she wanted to do was say something that would spook the nervous trio and send them scattering.

"Okay, why did you guys send me the tip about Kevin Cook?" Sophie asked. "And please, don't rush to talk at once."

Tina, sitting ramrod straight between Jimmy, who slouched in his seat, and Matt, who looked regretful and resigned, spoke up. "Because if anybody killed Eamon, it was Kevin."

"Cops arrested the wrong person," said Jimmy, head bent, eyes avoiding Sophie and Beanie.

"Who did the cops arrest?" Matt asked.

Noelle tensed. So far, because of Caleb Olivier's loyalty to Beanie and compassion toward their family, Noelle's name had been kept out of the *Palmchat Gazette*. The Palmchat Pharmacy human resources department had stayed quiet though they knew the details of her arrest. Noelle was grateful she'd been spared gawking, taunts, and salacious speculation about her guilt or innocence.

Beanie said, "They didn't arrest Kevin Cook. There's really no evidence against him."

"Unless you guys know something you should tell the police," Sophie said.

Shoulders slumped, Tina said, "After Eamon was killed, the three of us discussed who could have killed him and we all agreed—Kevin Cook."

"But why Kevin?" Beanie asked.

Matt said, "Kevin was really upset when Eamon got the Palmchat Pharmacy job."

"Upset?" Jimmy scoffed as he raised his head. "Understatement. Livid is the word. He hated that Dr. Bean gave Eamon the job."

"Kevin said Eamon didn't deserve the job," Tina said. "He said Eamon probably got the job because Eamon was good-looking and he probably—"

"Kevin was just saying Eamon shouldn't have gotten the job," Matt cut in, giving Tina a warning glance. "Kevin thought he was smarter than Eamon and—"

"What were you going to say, Tina?" asked Sophie. "You were saying that Kevin thought Eamon got the job because he was handsome and ... what else?"

Matt shook his head and crossed his arms, obviously peeved, which Sophie must have noticed because she asked, "Is there something you don't want Tina to tell me?"

"Not with Dr. Bean standing right there," said Matt. "She doesn't need to know about Kevin's bullshit theories because they're not true."

"I do want to know," said Noelle, breaking the vow she'd made to herself to stay quiet. "What is Kevin's bullshit theory?"

Beanie glanced back at her, his expression wary but Noelle concentrated on the trio as she took a few steps away from the lectern.

Tina said, "Kevin suggested that Eamon got the job because he and Dr. Bean were having an affair."

Noelle's legs shook, and she regretted her decision to leave the lectern, which she could have leaned on for the support she desperately needed at that moment.

"Kevin thought my wife and Eamon were having an affair?" Beanie asked, a hint of incredulity in his tone but Noelle heard the trace of rage, as well.

"We didn't believe it," Tina said, rolling her eyes. "Kevin was just pissed about Eamon getting the job. He couldn't believe that Eamon deserved the job and he was convinced that Eamon hadn't gotten the job because he was capable of doing it better than Kevin."

"Okay, so ..." Sophie paced a bit, arms folded. "What I'm hearing is a guy who was jealous and snarky. But that doesn't necessarily make Kevin a murderer."

"That's not all he said," said Jimmy.

"Maybe we shouldn't be talking about this," Matt said, worry in his gaze as he glanced at his cohorts. "I mean, we don't want to cause problems for Kevin especially since he's not the only one who could have killed Eamon."

"He's not?" Beanie asked.

"Who else could have killed Eamon?" asked Sophie.

"We should tell them about Sarah," Matt said.

"Sarah Linde?" Beanie frowned.

"What about Sarah?" Noelle asked.

"Sarah could have killed Eamon," Matt said.

Rolling her eyes, Tina said, "You can't seriously think that Sarah could have killed Eamon."

"She wrote those crazy letters," Matt said.

"What crazy letters?" asked Sophie.

"Sarah wrote Eamon some letters saying she would die if she couldn't be with him," said Jimmy. "Stupid lovesick shit."

"She also wrote in one of those letters that she would rip Eamon's heart out," said Matt.

"Yeah, she said she'd rip out his heart not bash him over the head," said Tina. "Sarah wasn't serious. She was just trying to get his attention."

"The letter said Sarah would rip Eamon's heart out?" asked Beanie, glancing at Noelle, his gaze conveying the disturbing realization she'd come to—Sarah Linde had written the threatening love letters the police had found in Eamon's apartment.

"Sarah can get a little obsessively possessive when she likes a guy," Tina said. "So, she was depressed and upset because she realized Eamon had used her for sex and wasn't really interested."

"Which could be a motive for murder," said Matt.

Tina shook her head. "You're just trying to deflect suspicion onto Sarah because you don't want to believe that Kevin killed Eamon."

Sophie said, "Jimmy, a few minutes ago, you were going to tell us something that Kevin had said, remember?"

"He said he wanted to kill Eamon," said Jimmy, frowning.

Matt exhaled, rubbing his jaw.

"It's true." Tina nodded. "We heard him say that."

"He didn't actually say he would kill Eamon," Matt disputed. "He didn't use the word kill."

"What word did he use?" Beanie asked.

"He said somebody should get Eamon out of our lives," said Matt, rushing the words out as though it pained him to say them. "But we didn't really think he was serious."

"Until Eamon was murdered," said Jimmy.

Sophie sighed. "I think we need to call the police."

"What? No, we can't do that," said Matt.

"We have to," said Jimmy.

"We don't have proof Kevin did anything," Matt pointed out. "Just because he said he wanted to get rid of Eamon doesn't mean he killed him."

"True, but the police should know that Kevin had animosity toward Eamon," said Sophie.

"She's right," said Tina, looking at Matt and then at Jimmy. "We owe it to Eamon to tell the cops what we know."

"Even if what we know may not be true?" Matt asked. "Don't we owe it to Kevin to hear what he has to say?"

Sophie pulled out her phone. "How about we let Kevin tell the police what he has to say for himself."

Chapter Forty-Two

Worried and apprehensive, Noelle leaned a hip against the kitchen counter.

She'd just managed to coax the boys to sleep after a fitful few hours during which Evan had been unusually fussy, and Ethan had been excessively rambunctious. There was peace in the house, finally, but discord churned in her gut.

Two days had passed since she, Beanie and Sophie had talked to the anonymous tipster. Or, rather, the anonymous tipsters—Tina, Matt, and Jimmy. Noelle was still having problems wrapping her mind around the idea that she and Beanie had been right.

Kevin Cook had killed Eamon and framed her for the murder.

Maybe.

Beanie was convinced of Kevin's guilt and had spent the past forty-eight hours harassing Officer Fields and Detective Janvier, demanding that they arrest Kevin Cook immediately. Officer Fields, who'd driven out to the university to take the interns' statements after Sophie's insistent phone call, had promised to interview Kevin Cook a second time, considering the new revelations, once Kevin returned to St. Killian.

Janvier was disinclined to believe that someone else had killed

Eamon Taylor. He was convinced Noelle had killed Eamon—even though Octavia's cousin Icarus had discovered that the burner used to send the lewd emails to Eamon had been purchased on the island of St. Cera on a date and at a time when Noelle had been working at the pharmacy.

According to Octavia, when presented with the evidence, Janvier wouldn't accept that it contradicted his theory of Noelle's motive for the murder. Janvier believed Noelle had arranged for someone to purchase the phone for her.

Janvier had told Octavia there was no evidence to support a theory of Kevin Cook as the killer. The doubts and suspicions of college students meant nothing to him.

Noelle had been disappointed, but part of her struggled to believe Kevin had killed Eamon, as well. Initially, when she and Beanie had first begun to suspect Kevin might be guilty, Noelle had wholeheartedly agreed. She'd been desperate to find the better suspect.

But *was* Kevin really the better suspect?

Thinking about it logically and objectively, Noelle didn't know. She wanted so much to believe in her heart Kevin was the killer, but as Janvier had said, where was the evidence? Kevin's girlfriend, Sarah, and three of his friends, Matt, Tina, and Jimmy, had each admitted to being suspicious of him. They all believed Kevin could have killed Eamon out of envy. They'd heard Kevin express animosity toward Eamon. *Saying he wanted to kill Eamon.* Although, as Matt had pointed out, Kevin might not have been serious. Had Kevin been jealous of Eamon? Probably. Envy didn't always lead to murder, though.

Noelle turned toward the window and stared at the rose bushes she needed to tend to.

It was possible that Kevin forced Sarah to create the 'doctor sexy MILF' email account so he could send fake emails to Eamon, but there was no proof. How did she know Sarah had been telling the truth about Kevin delivering a book to her? Maybe Kevin hadn't been in their home that night. Noelle didn't want to suspect Sarah, but after Tina's revelation about Sarah's secret relationship with Eamon, Noelle wasn't sure she could trust Sarah anymore.

Tina's description of Sarah as *obsessively possessive toward Eamon* made Noelle think of the love letter found in Eamon's apartment, one of the clues the cops had dismissed. Could Sarah have written the note? The letter had an obsessive tone and had mentioned death. *I'll rip your heart out.* Could Sarah have killed Eamon because he'd spurned her? Was a woman scorned capable of cold-blooded murder?

Noelle exhaled. The lack of physical evidence tying Kevin to the murder bothered her. The murder weapon—the shovel with the bent head—had Noelle's fingerprints on it. The body had been found in the trunk of her car.

Octavia had told them the police had found almost no trace evidence in Eamon's apartment. There were no fingerprints. No DNA. Nothing to really point the police away from her and toward someone else.

Had Kevin killed Eamon? Beanie always told her a suspect needed motive, means, and opportunity. Kevin's motive could have been envy. Kevin was certainly capable of beating Eamon to death with a shovel. But had Kevin had the opportunity to kill Eamon?

Kevin didn't have an alibi during the time Eamon had been killed. Sarah had admitted to Beanie and Sophie, and the cops, that Kevin had told her to say they'd been together the day Eamon had been killed but that wasn't true. So, where had Kevin been when Eamon was viciously murdered?

The phone rang.

Noelle started but was grateful for the interruption. She needed a break from the speculation and the dire directions of her thoughts. She didn't like doubting Sarah.

Grabbing the cordless receiver from the base on the breakfast peninsula, Noelle answered the landline.

"Dr. Bean ... it's Kevin Cook."

Noelle's heart sped up.

Kevin said, "I think we need to talk."

Chapter Forty-Three

Noelle took a deep breath. "What do we need to talk about?"

"About Eamon Taylor's murder," said Kevin. "I know you think I killed him but I didn't."

Noelle went to the table and sat. "Why do you think I think you killed Eamon?"

"I know that Tina, Matt, and Jimmy talked to you and your husband and that other reporter about me," said Kevin. "They told you that I was jealous of Eamon and—"

"How do you know we talked to them?" Noelle asked.

Silence.

Waiting for Kevin to respond, Noelle heard horns honking, the roar of engines, and the low hum of background conversation. Where was he?

"Matt told me," said Kevin. "He's the only one who has my back."

"Are you sure?" Noelle asked. "Matt said he heard you say you wanted to kill Eamon."

"Matt knows I was just mad about the Palmchat Pharmacy job."

"And about the fact that Sarah was cheating on you with Eamon," Noelle said.

"I didn't care about Sarah hooking up with Eamon," Kevin said.

"But Sarah is your girlfriend," said Noelle, shocked by Kevin's dismissive tone.

"Sarah isn't anybody's girlfriend." Kevin scoffed. "She's the pharmacy school bike, okay? Everybody's had a ride."

Offended by his sexist insults, Noelle said, "Sarah was at your apartment when my husband and his colleague went to talk to you about an anonymous tip they'd received."

"I know all about the anonymous tip," said Kevin. "It's not true. And as for Sarah being at my place, she offered to apartment-sit while I went to the seminar. I don't know what she told your husband about our relationship, but she lied."

"And did Sarah lie when she said you told her to lie to the police and tell them the two of you were together the say Eamon was killed?"

More silence.

"Kevin?" Noelle prompted.

"Sarah didn't lie about that," said Kevin. "I told her to give me an alibi because I didn't want the cops on my ass accusing me of something I didn't do."

Noelle didn't want the cops on her ass, either, but they were.

"So where were you when Eamon was killed?"

"At Cactus Beach," he said. "Smoking weed. And, no, nobody can back up my story. I went out there to relax and clear my mind. I was not bashing Eamon's head with a shovel and hacking his body into pieces. But, thanks to Tina, Sarah, Matt, and Jimmy, the cops want to talk to me."

"Maybe you should go to the police," Noelle encouraged.

"And tell them what? That there's no way I killed Eamon? They might not believe me," said Kevin, desperation, and fear sneaking into his tone. "They might have some evidence against me. Something somebody planted at my place to make me look guilty."

"Who would do something like that to you?" Noelle asked.

"Probably that bitch Sarah," said Kevin. "She fucks anything that moves, but she gets obsessive. Clingy. Possessive."

Possessively obsessive, Noelle thought, remembering Tina's judgment of Sarah.

"You ask me, Sarah could have killed Eamon," said Kevin. "She wrote him some letters. Creepy bullshit. Eamon showed me a few. I stole a couple to show to Matt. We had a good laugh. She was writing stuff like they could be together in death or some shit. Sarah really liked Eamon. He wasn't interested in anything except banging her."

Noelle cleared her throat. "Kevin, is this why you called me? You wanted to talk about—"

"The cops arrested you for Eamon's murder, didn't they?"

Saying nothing, Noelle tried to think over the roar in her head. How the hell did Kevin know about her arrest? Her name hadn't been listed in any of Caleb Olivier's articles.

"If you're wondering how I know," said Kevin, "it's because I have a friend who works in the HR department at Palmchat Pharmacy. She's the director's secretary. The cops think you killed Eamon because he was going to sue you for sexual harassment."

Noelle hesitated, not sure what to say.

"I know you didn't kill him," Kevin said. "But I know who did, and I can prove it."

"You know who killed Eamon Taylor?"

Kevin said, "It was the PC-5."

Her heart slamming, Noelle said, "How do you know that? What proof do you have?"

"I have to show you the proof, or you won't believe me," said Kevin. "Look, I just got back from St. Croix, and I'm at the airport now but meet me at my apartment in an hour."

Suspicion and apprehension flooded Noelle. "I don't think that's a good idea. Why don't we meet at—"

"My ride's here, so I have to go," said Kevin. "The proof you need to help your case is in my apartment. You want it? Then come get it ..."

Chapter Forty-Four

Raindrops sprinkled on the windshield of the SUV as Noelle pulled into a space in the parking lot in front of Kevin Cook's apartment building.

The sky overhead had darkened as she'd made the drive from Oyster Farms to Kevin's apartment, located in one of the neighborhoods surrounding the university. Thirty minutes ago, when she left the house, she'd done so with reluctance and apprehension.

Again, she was embarking on another potentially dangerous quest to prove she hadn't killed Eamon Taylor but what choice did she have? Noelle hadn't wanted to contend with Kevin Cook by herself. She'd hoped Beanie would be able to accompany her, but when she'd tried to reach him, he hadn't responded to any of her repeated attempts. Desperate, she'd called the *Palmchat Gazette* and had been told Beanie was covering a meeting at the mayor's office where all attendees were required to turn off their cell phones.

After calling her mother to watch the boys, Noelle left email and voicemail messages for Beanie and then headed out, promising her mother she would be back shortly.

Staring through the rain-streaked glass at the massive Colonial plantation home, Noelle tried to shake off the feelings of dread. Low dark thunderheads rolled across the sky, swallowing the blue skies and sunshine that had started the day. Was it a sign? Maybe she should turn around and go home? As she'd navigated the streets, she'd gone back and forth, from hesitation to determination. One second, she was convinced Kevin Cook was a liar trying to set her up and the next she was telling herself she had to get the proof Kevin claimed to have about the PC-5 killing Eamon.

Tapping her nails on the steering wheel, Noelle sighed.

Could the PC-5 have killed Eamon? She'd thought so herself, at one time. After her confrontation with Grady Palmer in the airport hangar, she'd abandoned that theory. But, then Octavia had informed them of the debt Eamon owed to the gang—a debt he'd been struggling to pay —and she had to revisit the theory.

Noelle's father had once been a fearsome PC-5 "collection special- ist," punishing those who were in arrears to the gang. When she'd been part of the gang, she heard stories of her father's brutality and his legend had afforded her grudging respect.

Her dad would know if the PC-5 killed Eamon. Josue Chartres was behind bars, though, and Noelle didn't want to see him. The father who'd rarely been in her life might have the answers she needed but asking for Josue's help was a risk she probably shouldn't take.

Resolved to push away her fears, Noelle exited the SUV and dashed through the pattering rain to the main double doors of the large house. Before she lost her nerve, she pressed the buzzer for Kevin's apartment.

Thinking of risks she probably shouldn't take, meeting Kevin alone was definitely one. Beanie would be pissed when he found out but she was here now, and the door had just opened. Noelle entered the foyer. Though the home had been renovated into apartments, there were still remnants of its function as the massive mansion of an upper echelon colonist, his family and an army of indentured servants.

Heading up the stairway, Noelle felt the fear and panic slipping away and being replaced by the Handweg attitude. Once, she'd been a badass, and maybe it was time to call up those old reserves she'd tried so hard to pretend she'd never relied on. She couldn't let Kevin Cook scare her. Maybe he had killed Eamon, and he was trying to set her up, and if that was true, she supposed it wouldn't hurt to let him know she wasn't weak and spineless. In the past, she had to fight for herself because there was no one else to fight for her, and if she didn't fight, she wouldn't survive.

Chapter Forty-Five

As he walked into the *Palmchat Gazette* newsroom, Beanie stared at his cell phone, his apprehension growing as he stared at the missed texts from Noelle.

At his desk, Beanie found a message put there by the receptionist. *Noelle called. Urgent that you call her back ASAP.*

"Another snorefest at the mayor's budget meeting?" asked Stevie, taking a seat on the corner of Beanie's desk. "Glad I don't have to cover that boring crap. All that droning on and on about ..."

Barely registering Stevie's remarks, Beanie dropped into his creaky leather chair and accessed the first text Noelle had sent an hour ago. *Where are you? Need to talk to you about Kevin Cook. Important. Call me back.*

Ten minutes later, another text from Noelle read: *Why aren't you answering your phone? Kevin claims PC5 killed Eamon and he has proof. Wants to meet at his apartment.*

Fifteen minutes and then another text: *Called mom to watch the boys while I go to Kevin's. call me or meet me there.*

"Shit!" Beanie slammed his fist on the desk. "Why the hell would she do this again after what happened the last time?"

Stevie jumped. "What's the matter?"

"No time to explain." Beanie jumped up and strode around his desk. "Do me a favor, Stevie?"

Nodding, Stevie said, "What do you need?"

"Can I borrow your car?"

Stevie gaped at him. "My 'rari?"

"Never mind." Beanie cursed under his breath. He'd forgotten that Stevie drove an impossibly impractical Italian sports car. "I'll borrow Caleb's. He around?"

"Breakroom," said Stevie. "Hey, what's going on?"

"Call Officer Fields at the police department," said Beanie, dictating the instructions over his shoulder as he hurried toward the employee lounge. "I need him to meet me at Kevin Cook's apartment. He'll know the address. Tell him it could be a matter of life and death."

"Life and death?" asked Stevie as he followed Beanie.

Stopping abruptly, Beanie faced Stevie whose stricken panicked expression mirrored the emotions Beanie struggled to control. "My wife is going to get herself killed ..."

Chapter Forty-Six

Three quick, firm knocks on Kevin's attic apartment, and the door opened.

Noelle stepped back, startled.

"Hi, Dr. Bean."

"Matt?" Noelle was confused. "What are you doing here? Is Kevin around?"

"Kevin asked me to pick him up from the airport," explained Matt, switching his backpack from one shoulder to the other. "He's in the study back there. Down the hall, second door on the right."

"Thanks," said Noelle, noting Matt's anxious expression and the way he seemed to be avoiding her gaze. He'd displayed the same nervousness at the Collister building, when he, Tina, and Jimmy had announced themselves, collectively, as the anonymous tipster.

"Well, um, I have a lab ..." Matt cleared his throat and stepped over the threshold. "So, I guess I'll see you."

"Matt, wait," said Noelle, placing a hand on his arm to stop him. "Did you tell Kevin about the anonymous tips to the *Palmchat Gazette*."

Shoulders lumping, Matt exhaled. "Only because I didn't want him to be blindsided when the cops came to talk to him."

Nodding, Noelle said, "So, you gave him a heads up?"

"I don't think he killed Eamon Taylor," said Matt, his voice low and a bit defensive. "I don't care what Tina and Jimmy said. Kevin didn't do it. Whoever killed Eamon is probably somebody we don't even know. The guy did have a life away from the university. And I don't mean to say bad stuff about the dead, but he was from a bad neighborhood. He could have been mixed up with criminals. How do we know? People don't tell you everything about themselves."

"You're right," said Noelle, thinking of the things her friends and colleagues didn't know about her and the secrets about her past she'd kept from Beanie.

"Anyway, like I said, Kevin's in the study." His expression sullen, Matt walked away from her and headed down the stairs.

Stepping into Kevin's apartment, Noelle felt the fear and panic returning. She should have asked Matt to stay with her while she talked to Kevin. More and more, she was starting to believe Kevin wasn't the killer, but her apprehension was still strong as she took a few tentative steps into the spacious living area. Like most plantation homes from the early eighteenth century, the attic was large and roomy with slightly above average ceilings. Attics had often been used as servants' quarters or storage rooms where large quantities of household supplies were kept.

Turning, Noelle went back to the door. She couldn't leave it open, but she didn't want to be closed in the apartment with Kevin. She decided to leave the door open a crack. She hoped Kevin would be quick about showing her the proof, but she couldn't rule out that he might have tricked her into coming to his apartment to try to hurt her. She couldn't ignore Beanie's belief that Kevin had killed Eamon Taylor and Ted Chen. If that turned out to be true, and she had to run for her life, Noelle didn't want a closed and locked door to become an obstacle.

Anxious to uncover the proof Kevin claimed to have, Noelle headed to the study and knocked on the door, which was opened slightly. She called out to Kevin and then pushed the door open. The room, which had probably originally been a bedroom, was empty but she heard the shower going behind a door in the corner.

For a moment, Noelle wondered why Kevin would jump in the

shower when he knew she was coming to talk about his proof, but she remembered the end of their conversation. She hadn't confirmed that she would meet him. For all Kevin knew, she could have decided she didn't believe him.

Her phone vibrated, and she pulled it from the purse hanging from her shoulder. A text. Hoping it was from Beanie, she accessed it. Realizing it was from Sarah Linde, Noelle tempered her disappointment and irritation. The things she'd recently learned about Sarah were disturbing. Noelle's opinion of the babysitter had soured, but she couldn't be judgmental and hypocritical, especially considering her own secrets.

Reading the text, Noelle frowned.

dr. bean its sarah just remembering something. The night when kevin came to give me the book i needed matt was with him. Maybe matt used your computer?

Interesting, but Noelle wasn't shocked because Matt and Kevin were good friends. Could Kevin have directed Matt to create the fake email accounts? Possibly, but if so, then Noelle would have to revisit, again, the theory that Kevin was the killer and had set her up. She was still struggling to view Kevin as the killer so how could she think he'd convinced Matt to do his dirty work?

Exhaling, Noelle glanced toward the shower as she crossed the room to a bookshelf.

She suspected Eamon Taylor had directed Sarah Linde to create the fake email account. And now, Sarah was probably panicking, probably afraid of someone uncovering her part in Eamon's scam.

Noelle was convinced Eamon had put a plan in motion to extort money from her by claiming she'd sexually harassed him. Obviously, Eamon had recognized Sarah's obsession with him and had taken advantage of it. He'd manipulated Sarah into helping him, but when he wouldn't return Sarah's affections, the young woman had killed him.

After her talk with Kevin, Noelle planned to stop by Octavia's suite at the Queen Palm. Hopefully, Kevin's proof would be substantial and would also support Noelle's theory about Sarah Linde as Eamon's killer.

Noelle accessed the recording app on her phone—one of Beanie's journalism tricks—and placed the phone on the second highest shelf. Kevin wouldn't notice it, but their conversation would be recorded loud and clear for Octavia and the police.

Lightening flashed, and the subsequent crash of thunder made Noelle gasp. Rubbing her arms, she walked to the closed bathroom door. Kevin was certainly taking a long shower. Should she knock? Admonishing herself to be patient, she turned.

Matt loomed in front of her, his expression as cold and menacing as the gun he pointed at her.

Chapter Forty-Seven

"Sit down, Dr. Bean," ordered Matt.

Confused and terrified, Noelle followed his directive, backing toward the couch. Wary, watching him, she sank down on the cushioned seat. What the hell was happening? Why was Matt pointing a gun at her? Nothing made sense. Why had Matt come back into the apartment? He'd told her he was leaving to go to a class. Why would he come back with a gun? Had Kevin told him to pull a gun on her?

Noelle wrestled with emotions threatening to overwhelm her. She'd made another dangerous mistake, coming to see Kevin alone. The worse part was she'd known she was doing something foolish, but she'd done it anyway. Once again, thinking she was still badass, she'd put her life in grave danger.

"Finally, me and you, bitch," said Matt, giving her a cruel smirk.

"Where is Kevin?"

"Forget about him," said Matt. "Kevin is no longer with us."

"Kevin!" Noelle screamed, panic exploding within her. "Kevin, help—"

"Shut up!" Matt roared, and with two long strides, the gun was inches from her face. "Kevin can't help you, Dr. Bean. He never could and now he never will."

"What does that mean?"

"He's dead."

Noelle's stomach lurched. "What? No ... the shower ..."

"Oh, I left it running after I got out of it," said Matt with a shrug and a chuckle. "There was a lot of blood. I had to wash it all off me. Couldn't walk around looking like Carrie."

Shivering, Noelle shook her head.

"What? Don't believe me?" Matt asked. "Take a look for yourself."

Noelle froze.

"Go ahead, Dr. Bean," encouraged Matt. "Look in the bathroom, and you'll see I'm telling the truth."

Shaking her head, Noelle said, "No, I don't—"

"Do it!" Matt ordered, his harsh command followed by more booming thunder. "Get up and go look in the bathroom and you will see that I am telling the truth!"

Noelle stood. Legs shaking, she side-stepped to the bathroom door. Her mind whirled with thoughts of escape. She had to get out of Kevin's apartment. She couldn't let Matt kill her but he had a gun, and he was blocking her pathway out of the study.

"Open the damn door!"

Jumping, Noelle complied. The door swung back, and she stifled a scream, pressing a palm against her mouth, trying not to vomit. Blood was everywhere—splashed and splattered all over the washbasin and toilet and the shower, still sending a fine steamy spray into the tub.

Kevin Cook was drowned in blood. Pooling beneath his pale, naked body, the blood seeped from several deep, mangled stabs slashed across his face, throat, chest, and thighs.

Noelle slammed the door shut on the gruesome scene and faced Matt. "Why would you kill Kevin? He's your friend."

"Kevin is an ungrateful asshole," raged Matt. "I pick him up from the airport and how does he thank me? He accuses me of killing Eamon and claims to have proof which he won't show the police if I give him an exorbitant amount of money. Can you believe the bastard tried to blackmail me? That wasn't the original plan. The original plan was to blackmail you."

"Blackmail me? I don't understand?"

"Because you're a dumb, clueless bitch, that's why you don't under-stand," said Matt. "But I'll explain. I picked Kevin up from the airport, and he gets in the car with this idea to extort money from you using some evidence he supposedly has that the PC-5 killed Eamon."

"That's why I came here," said Noelle. "Kevin said he had proof that the PC-5 killed Eamon. If I wanted the proof, I had to come to his apartment and get it."

"He didn't lie to you," said Matt. "He did have proof. A letter from one of Eamon's old girlfriends. She warned Eamon that he was on the PC-5 death list, whatever the hell that is."

Noelle knew about the dreaded death list. Each week, PC-5 enforcers were given a list of names, targets they were responsible for taking care of, people who had incurred the wrath of the gang and had been marked for death.

Noelle had once seen her father drawing lines through the names of the people he'd killed. Later, when she was a teenager, she'd learned the grisly red smears had been the blood of his victims, a horrific PC-5 requirement.

"Anyway, Kevin was supposed to blackmail you," said Matt. "But then he wanted to blackmail me, too."

"How was he going to blackmail you?"

"Kevin found my manifesto."

Noelle shivered as she stared into Matt's cold eyes. "Your manifesto?"

Shrugging, Matt said, "I had a notebook where I wrote down how I planned to kill Eamon and blame you for it. Two birds, one stone, I titled it. I must have left the notebook here or something. Kevin read it and made copies. Then he tells me that I can pay him for the copies or he'll give them to the cops for free."

"That's why you killed him."

"Actually," said Matt. "I killed Kevin because he was an arrogant, lazy, entitled bastard who thought he was smarter than everybody, but that wasn't true. Kevin was not the smartest. And Eamon sure as hell wasn't. I, Matthew Delaney, am the smartest and everyone knows that but they won't admit it."

Shrinking back against the couch, Noelle tried to think of a way to escape, but Matt's deranged expression and psychotic ranting was paralyzing.

"I, Matthew Delaney, am the smartest," Matt raved on, "but for some reason, you didn't see that. You didn't want to see it. I am the one who deserved the job at Palmchat Pharmacy because I'm smarter than Eamon and Kevin and Sarah and Tina and Jimmy and all the rest of them! But you didn't want to admit that, Dr. Bean. All you wanted to see was Eamon Taylor. Good-looking Eamon! That dumbass island thug gets the job over me because you want to bang his brains out!"

Noelle shook her head. "That's not true."

"Isn't it?" Matt cocked his head. "You sent him all those disgusting emails telling him how bad you wanted him to be inside you."

"I never sent those emails," said Noelle, covertly trying to glance around the room, scanning for a weapon, anything she could use to get away.

Matt laughed. "Yeah, I know, you didn't send them. I sent them to Eamon for you."

"You created that fake *doctor sexy MILF* account on my home computer," said Noelle, burgeoning anger joining her terror.

"It was perfect serendipity," said Matt. "I couldn't believe it when Kevin asked me to drive him to your house to drop off a book for that slut Sarah. By the way, they screwed on your couch."

Noelle glanced at the desk adjacent to the sofa. In addition to several large, heavy-looking books, there was a stapler and a coffee mug used as a pencil holder. The scissors in the mug might be useful, she thought. But how to get to them without getting shot in the back?

"Anyway, as I was saying," Matt said. "While Sarah was going down on Kevin, I went into your home office and created the account. So fortuitous! I knew I wanted to create the account from your computer and I thought I'd have to break into your house just like I broke into your garden shed and stole your shovel. Perfect murder weapon, by the way."

Noelle pressed her lips together. Everything within her compelled her to lunge at Matt and go for his throat, but she had to be calm. She had to get out of the situation alive if she had any chance of giving

Matt's confession to the police. She hadn't forgotten about her phone on the bookshelf. The recording app didn't have a limit, and it was a small comfort, knowing it was taping every one of Matt's sick, twisted words.

"I can't believe you killed Eamon," said Noelle.

"I can't believe you didn't figure it out," Matt said. "On second thought, I can believe you didn't figure it out. Anyway, Eamon got what he deserved because you gave him what he didn't deserve. You gave him that job because you felt sorry for him. Both of you are from the wrong side of the island, so you wanted to help one of your own, which was wrong because in doing so, you screwed me out of what I deserved."

"And you set it up to look like I had killed Eamon."

Matt rolled his eyes. "Duh ... of course, I set you up. And I know it worked. The cops arrested you. Nothing was said in the *Palmchat Gazette*, but it was all part of the public record, so I searched the criminal court database using your name and found a record of your bail hearing. And why would you need a bail hearing? Only because you must have been arrested."

"Why?" Noelle asked, confused by Matt's motive. "Why kill Eamon because he got a job you wanted? Did you think you couldn't get a job somewhere else?"

"He's not dead because he was given a job I wanted," said Matt, teeth clenched. "He's dead because he got what he didn't deserve. I should have gotten that job. It's not right for people to get special favors. People shouldn't get what they don't deserve. They shouldn't benefit from perks and unfair advantages. You should only get what you have worked diligently to attain. Otherwise, it's ill-gotten."

"But, do you really think Eamon deserved to die because he got a job you thought he wasn't the most qualified for?"

"When Eamon got the job he didn't deserve," said Matt, "I got humiliation I didn't deserve. Everyone knew the job should have been mine. I got all these sad, apologetic looks. I was mortified. And it was your fault because you were too stupid to give the job to the person who really deserved it!"

Thunder crashed, shaking the attic as Matt glared at her, his eyes wide and rabid, nostrils flaring, mouth twisted into a tight scowl.

"Eamon is dead because of your bad decisions!" Matt said, the gun shaking in his trembling hand. "If you had done the right thing and given me the job then Eamon would be alive! Eamon's blood is on your hands!"

Chapter Forty-Eight

After banging his fist against the buzzer for what seemed like forever, the main door opened, and Beanie rushed up the stairs to Kevin Cook's attic apartment. Dripping wet from the downpour he'd dashed through after exiting Caleb Olivier's station wagon, he slipped on one of the steps. Grabbing the railing, he continued his frantic ascent, eyes trained on the second staircase leading to the landing outside Kevin's place.

The disappointed anger he'd felt toward Noelle for her knee-jerk reactionary decisions had dissipated as he sped along the curving roads, praying he wouldn't have an accident, begging God to let him get to Noelle in time.

Before that psychotic bastard, Kevin Cook killed her.

That story Kevin had given her about having proof that the PC-5 had killed Eamon was a trap. There was no such proof. The PC-5 hadn't ordered Eamon's death. Kevin Cook had killed Eamon just like he'd killed Ted Chen and was now planning to kill Noelle.

Why the hell had Noelle believed that son of a bitch?

Taking the steps two at a time, Beanie reached the alcove of Kevin's apartment. Staring at the door, he felt his heart slamming. The door was half-opened. His instincts pushed him to rush into the apartment. Logic told him to be smart. He needed to be careful if he was going to get Noelle out of the apartment alive.

Officer Fields had been out when Stevie called, but the desk sergeant promised to radio Fields and give him the message. Beanie had called Octavia to keep her in the loop. As soon as her cousin Icarus returned to the hotel suite, she promised to send him to Kevin's apartment. She was also going to keep trying to reach Officer Fields.

Slipping into the doorway, Beanie knew he couldn't rely on anyone except himself to save Noelle.

Glancing around the living room, he searched for signs of struggle or trauma. Continuing down the hall toward the bedrooms, he stopped. What was that noise? Voices? Was someone talking? A man. Kevin Cook? Had to be. Staying close to the wall, Beanie inched closer to the bedrooms ...

Chapter Forty-Nine

"You're insane," said Noelle.

"Technically, maybe," said Matt, shrugging. "I was tested as a child after my mother caught me trying to strangle the cat."

Horrified, Noelle cut her eyes to the scissors on the desk as desperation flooded her. As much as she wanted to grab her phone with Matt's recorded confession, Noelle had decided she would leave it behind if she had to. Getting away from Matt was paramount. She would worry about the evidence once she was away from him and safe.

"They put me on anti-psychotic drugs, and I did well," said Matt. "Eventually, I was able to do okay without the meds. But then this travesty with Eamon kind of rocked my world. Anyway, enough with my villain's soliloquy. After all, this is not a mystery novel."

Taking a deep breath, Noelle tried to judge the distance from the couch to the desk.

"Time for you to die, Dr. Bean," said Matt.

Noelle cut her gaze to him. "Matt, you don't have to kill me. I won't tell anyone what you did. I promise. And, you know, Eamon's position will have to be filled, and I will give you the job if—"

"You think I'm stupid, Dr. Bean?" Matt glared at her. "You really think I believe that if I let you go, you won't tell the cops and you'll give me the job you should have given me in the first place? I'm crazy, not dumb! Didn't I tell you that I am the smartest? I'm smarter than Eamon, Kevin, Tina, Sarah, Jimmy and even you, Dr. Bean."

"Matt, please—"

"Shut up! Forget about begging for your life," he said. "It's pathetic, and it won't work. I don't care that your kids will grow up without a mother, or whatever you think might convince me to let you go."

Noelle choked back a sob, thinking of Ethan and Evan.

"So, here's what is going to happen, Dr. Bean," said Matt. "You are going to write a suicide note."

"A suicide note?" Noelle's heart kicked. "I'm not committing suicide."

"Well, no, you're not really going to commit suicide," said Matt. "I'm going to kill you, but I'm going to shoot you, so it appears you shot yourself. And then the cops will find the suicide note, written in your own words of how you killed Eamon Taylor, Ted Chen, and Kevin Cook. Don't worry; I'll dictate what you need to put in the note."

Her mind spinning, Noelle took small breaths, trying to think.

Matt Delaney was going to kill her if she didn't think of a way to get away from him. The suicide note might be her chance. Maybe when she was writing the note, she could use the pen to—

"Get the hell away from my wife!"

Chapter Fifty

Noelle screamed.

Shock, fear, and confusion seized her as she stared at the scene before her.

With a lunging leap, Beanie grabbed Matt Delaney in a grappling hold and slammed him to the floor. Wrestling on the carpet, Beanie and Matt struggled to trade punches as each of them fought to get the upper hand. Grunting and cursing, they rolled across the floor. When Matt ended up on top of Beanie, trying to choke him with his free hand, Noelle jumped up from the couch. Circling the study, looking for a weapon to help Beanie. Praying her husband wouldn't be shot, Noelle dashed to the desk and grabbed a massive Webster's dictionary.

Turning back to the fray, Noelle gasped.

Matt still had his hand around Beanie's throat while her husband tried to push the psychotic intern away from him. Her heart racing wildly, Noelle rushed into the melee, desperate to protect her husband, the father of her children, the man she would love forever.

Hoisting the dictionary in the air, Noelle brought it down against Matt's head.

Roaring in pain, Matt twisted his neck, looking over his shoulder at her. "You fucking bit—"

"Crazy asshole!" Noelle whacked him across the face, stumbling and tripping over legs as the tome fell from her hands. Unable to keep her balance, Noelle slid across the floor and fell to her hands and knees. She crawled in a circle until she faced Beanie and Matt.

Her husband was back in control, with his knee in Matt's chest. Pinning the intern against the floor, Beanie had the gun Matt had planned to kill her with and was slamming the butt of it against Matt's head, over and over until Matt went limp beneath him.

"Beanie ..." Noelle cried as she lurched to her feet.

Rising from Matt's unconscious form, Beanie stumbled to Noelle and wrapped his arms around her.

"Oh, God, Beanie ... " Noelle wrapped her arms around him, clinging tightly to him. "Oh, thank God, you're here! You came for me!"

"It's okay, Elle ... " Beanie whispered, soothingly, rubbing his hands up and down her back. "I'm here now. I'll always be here. I'm never leaving."

Sobbing, Noelle stared at him. "I'm so sorry, Beanie. I'm sorry I went off alone again! I should have never—"

"It's fine, Elle," Beanie said.

"I could have been killed," said Noelle, as the realization hit her hard. "I would never have seen you or the boys again! Why did I—"

"Elle, you're okay now. I am here. But you need to tell me what the hell happened?" Beanie placed both hands on her face, staring at her. "What is going on? Why was Matt Delany here? Why—"

"He killed Eamon Taylor," Noelle said, crying. "And Ted Chen ... and Kevin—"

Beanie grabbed her hands. "Kevin Cook is dead?"

Nodding, Noelle said, "It was so awful, he—"

"It's okay, babe ... " Beanie pulled her into his arms again. "The cops are coming. Officer Fields is on his way, and Octavia knows—"

"Beanie, I have to tell you something ... " Noelle pulled away to look up at him. "Matt Delaney admitted everything he did, and I recorded the conversation."

"You did?" A tentative smile played at the corner of Beanie's mouth. "Elle, how?"

"I used the recording app on my phone," said Noelle. "Just like you told me to do when we called Sarah."

Kissing her forehead, Beanie said, "Look at you being a junior investigative reporter. You ready for a byline a the *Palmchat Gazette*?"

Noelle sighed. "No, don't think I want to—"

"*STUPID BITCH DIE*!" Beneath the crashing thunder reverberating throughout the room, the words were like a curse from the deepest, blackest bowels of hell.

Paralyzed, Noelle tried to break through the fog of confusion and fear clouding her mind as she felt her body flying through the air. Landing on her side, Noelle scrambled to her hands and knees. Before her, Matt Delaney stood in front of Beanie, who was down on his left knee with his right leg extended, trying to get up.

His arm extended in the air, Matt growled as he slashed a butcher's knife down toward Beanie.

"Beanie!" Noelle screamed as the blade sliced against Beanie's forearm. "No!"

Beanie swept his extended leg toward Matt's foot. Stumbling, Matt swung the knife again, slashing Beanie's shoulder. Grunting in pain, Beanie kicked Matt's shin. Matt staggered to the side and dropped to his knees. Beanie took advantage and lunged at him.

Noelle stood and scanned the room for another weapon. Something heavier than the dictionary that had only knocked Matt out temporarily. Something more deadly.

Glancing at her husband and the psychotic intern, Noelle felt her heart drop. Matt had a death grip on the knife as he held it inches from Beanie's face. Beanie had his hand on Matt's wrist, his arm shaking as he tried to keep Matt from slashing him to ribbons.

Focusing herself, Noelle swept her gaze around the room again.

Gasping in relief, she stared at the couch. The gun Matt had planned to kill her with lay on the floor near the corner of the couch. With the grunts and groans of Beanie and Matt cutting through the roar of thunder, Noelle dived for the gun. Grabbing the pistol, Noelle rose to her knees and turned toward Beanie and Matt, both of them still wrestling for control of the knife.

"Get away from him!" Noelle screamed, training the gun on Matt, remembering the lessons she'd learned from her father—how to hold a gun, how to fire a pistol, how to hit her target. "Get back now, or I will shoot you!"

"Elle, no!" Beanie's head whipped toward her. "Stay back! Don't—"

Matt yanked his wrist from Beanie's grasp and then stabbed the knife into Beanie's chest.

Screaming her horror, Noelle squeezed the trigger.

Beneath the roll of thunder and the flash of lightning, the gun went off. Once, twice. Over and over, Noelle squeezed the trigger until the last bullet slammed into Matt's lifeless body.

Chapter Fifty-One

Noelle opened the door to the hospital room, stepped inside, and paused.

Tears pricked her eyes as she stared at the most beautiful sight in the world. The three most precious, most important things to her—Beanie and their boys.

Quietly closing the door behind her, Noelle tipped to the chair in the corner and sank into the plush leather. Sunlight from the twelve-paned picture window cast a golden glow over her husband, his arms around Ethan, who snuggled next to him, and Evan, secure in the baby pouch carefully strapped over Beanie's good shoulder.

At nine in the morning, her three favorite guys were still sleeping, but Noelle didn't mind.

After everything they'd all been through, Beanie deserved the rest and the unconditional love and affection from their boys.

Tucking her legs beneath her, Noelle glanced toward the window, watching the tall palms swaying in the breeze.

Four days had passed since the awful events in Kevin Cook's apartment.

After Noelle had fired the last shot, things had passed in a sickening blur. Dropping the gun, she'd run to Beanie and dropped to her knees next to him. Horrified by the blood spreading across his chest, Noelle had ripped his shirt open, searching for the wound, desperate to stop the bleeding.

Officer Fields and several other deputies had arrived. As the police crowded the room, Noelle screamed at them to call an ambulance.

Moments later, Noelle was at the hospital praying that Beanie would make it through surgery. The blade had missed the major organs, but Beanie had lost a lot of blood. Octavia had been there for support and to inform her that the police believed she'd shot Matt in self-defense.

She wouldn't be charged for killing the psychotic intern.

The next day, as Beanie recovered from his wounds, Octavia had even better news.

While processing the crime scene, the police had recovered Noelle's cell phone which had Matt Delaney's confession. Also, after a search of Matt's apartment, the police had physical evidence linking Matt to murders of Eamon Taylor, Ted Chen, and Kevin Cook.

They also had the notebook Kevin Cook had found—Matt's rambling manifesto of his hate and resentment toward Eamon Taylor and Noelle. Incensed when he didn't get the Palmchat Pharmacy job, Matt had outlined his plans to make the two of them pay.

"Hey, hot mama …"

Noelle looked over at Beanie. "Hey, sugar daddy," she teased, adding a wink.

"Sugar daddy?" Beanie snickered. "Don't make me laugh, Elle. I'm only two years older than you."

Noelle said, "I meant to say, hey handsome hero."

Beanie's grin faltered as he shook his head. "The hero usually doesn't end up with a knife in his chest."

"He does if he puts himself in harm's way to save the damsel in distress."

"That deranged bastard put you through more than just distress," said Beanie, scowling. "He was going to kill you."

"But he didn't because of you," said Noelle.

"And because of you," said Beanie, "he'll never hurt us, or anyone else again."

Noelle looked down. Shooting Matt wasn't something she'd wanted to do, or was proud of, but she didn't regret putting several bullets in him. She would do it again if it meant saving Beanie's life. She'd squeezed the trigger to protect her future, to make sure her boys would grow up with their father, and to stop a psychotic killer from getting away with murder.

"Come over here," said Beanie.

Her heart soaring with love, Noelle stood and walked to the hospital bed. She lifted Evan from the pouch, cradled him in her arms, and then carefully sat down on the bed and maneuvered her body next to Beanie's.

"Not that I want to talk about that demented asshole," said Beanie, "but did Octavia say anything about the charges against you?"

Noelle smiled. "I talked to her last night. Janvier recommended that the murder charges against me be dropped, and the prosecutor agreed."

"So, that means you are officially innocent," said Beanie, beaming. "You're not going to jail for a crime you didn't commit."

"And I have more good news," said Noelle, bending to kiss Ethan, and then Beanie, and finally, Evan. "I'm not going to lose my job. I've been officially reinstated, and I'm going back to work next week."

"I told you the nightmare would end," said Beanie. "From now on, it's going to be sweet dreams."

Hey there, it's Noelle Bean ...

Thank you for reading my story ... The Unworthy Wife.

When my past came back to haunt me in the worst possible way, I'll admit that I panicked.

I was so terrified of losing everything I'd worked so hard for, everything I didn't believe I deserved, that I felt I had no choice but to do whatever it took to protect my family—even if it meant lying to my loving, faithful husband, Beanie.

When I was falsely accused of murder, I thought I would lose my mind. Some of the choices I made could have gotten me killed, but I was so determined to clear my name that I didn't consider the danger.

Now I realize that I never should have lied to my husband. Beanie is my rock and I should have leaned on him and allowed him to help me from the beginning.

Thankfully, I came to my senses, told my husband the truth, and together, we faced one of the greatest adversities in our marriage.

We were tested and tried, and we made it.

Hopefully, you'll learn something from my mistakes and you'll never doubt, like I did, that you deserve love, support, compassion, and respect.

If you enjoyed my tale of regret to redemption, then I'm sure you'll love the story of Quinn Miller ... The Perfect Liar.

Much like me, Quinn is a strong, capable woman who makes some disastrous choices when she finds herself frustrated and unsure of where to turn.

When Quinn's life spins out of control, she decides to visit a very unique hotel where all of her secret desires and forbidden fantasies are catered to by a bevy of hunky guys.

Unfortunately, Quinn's fantasy turns into a nightmare when she is targeted by a shady blackmailer with deadly intent.

Quinn's story is full of danger, intrigue ... and sex.

You'll be hooked from the first page!

Click here to get your copy of The Perfect Liar now.

Best,

Noelle

Rachel Woods has been entertaining readers with her brand of romantic mystery suspense -- sexy dangerous fiction. Now you can get one of her short stories for FREE, when you sign up to join her newsletter:

GET MY FREE SHORT STORY NOW

https://BookHip.com/HAGPDF

Also by Rachel Woods

REPORTER ROLAND BEAN COZY MYSTERIES

Roland "Beanie" Bean, husband and loving father, finds himself the unwitting participant in solving crimes as he seeks to make a name for himself as a reporter for the *Palmchat Gazette*.

EASTER EGG HUNT MURDER

MERRY CHRISTMAS MURDER

TRICK OR TREAT MURDER

PALMCHAT ISLANDS MYSTERIES

Married journalists, Vivian and Leo, manage the island newspaper while solving crimes as they chase leads for their next story.

THE SILENT ENEMY

THE BLOODSTAINED BRIDE

THE PRODIGAL CAPTIVE

THE VENGEFUL CALLER

THE SHAMEFUL ACCUSER

THE PALMCHAT ISLANDS MYSTERIES BOX SET: BOOKS 1 - 5

SPENCER & SIONE SERIES

Gripping romantic suspense series with steamy romance, unpredictable plot twists and devastating consequences of deceit.

FLAWLESS MISTAKE

FLAWLESS DANGER

FLAWLESS BETRAYAL

THE SPENCER & SIONE COLLECTION BOX SET: BOOKS 1 - 3

STAND-ALONE BOOKS

Stand-alone romantic mystery novels all set in the fictional Palmchat Islands.

THE UNWORTHY WIFE

THE PERFECT LIAR

Also by Angel Vane

The Hidden Threat
The Accidental Hero
The Unworthy Wife
The Silent Enemy

About the Author ~ Rachel Woods

Rachel Woods studied journalism and graduated from the University of Houston where she published articles in the Daily Cougar. She is a legal assistant by day and a freelance writer and blogger with a penchant for melodrama by night. Many of her stories take place on the islands, which she has visited around the world. Rachel resides in Houston, Texas with her three sock monkeys.

For more information:
www.therachelwoods.com
rachel@therachelwoods.com

facebook.com/therachelwoodsauthor

instagram.com/therachelwoodsauthor

bookbub.com/authors/rachel-woods

amazon.com/author/therachelwoods

About the Author ~ Angel Vane

Angel Vane has a dramatic personality, is prone to exaggeration and is in perpetual pursuit of her creative muse. She loves writing, reading, traveling, spa days and soap operas. Angel resides in Tomball, Texas.

For more information:
angelvaneauthor@gmail.com

About the Publisher

BonzaiMoon Books is a family-run, artisanal publishing company created in the summer of 2014. We publish works of fiction in various genres. Our passion and focus is working with authors who write the books you want to read, and giving those authors the opportunity to have more direct input in the publishing of their work.

To receive special offers, bonus content and news about our latest ebooks, sign up for our mailing list on our website.

For more information:
www.bonzaimoonbooks.com
bonzaimoon@gmail.com

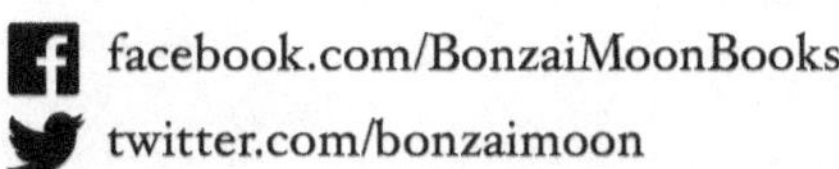

www.ingramcontent.com/pod-product-compliance
Lightning Source LLC
Chambersburg PA
CBHW030623190726
48286CB00008B/2366